circling the tortilla dragon

circling the tortilla dragon

SHORT-SHORT FICTIONS RAY GONZALEZ

CREATIVE ARTS BOOK COMPANY
Berkeley 🐉 California

For information contact:
Creative Arts Book Company
833 Bancroft Way
Berkeley, California 94710
www.creativeartsbooks.com

The characters, places, incidents and situations in this book are imaginary and have no relation to any person, place or actual happening.

The author thanks the editors of the following publications where some of these pieces first appeared:
The Bitter Oleander: "The Last Mayan Indian"; *Bellevue Literary Review:* "The Old Man Who Combed His Hair"; *Colere:* "Historical Marker"; *Flyway Literary Review:* "Collecting Parrots"; *Humor By Writers of Color: An Anthology* (University of Iowa Press): "The Glass Eye," "Komodo Dragon," "Mistakes," and "Pyramid"; *Indiana Review:* "Juarez Bees"; *LIT Magazine:* "The Spy"; *LUNA:* "The Jukebox"; *Many Mountains Moving:* "The Church"; *Opening the Center: An Anthology of Short Fiction* (Red Hen Press): "The Crucifix is Down"; *Portland Review:* "The Walls"; *The Prose Poem:* "Busy"; *The Raven Chronicles:* "Metaphysical Light"; *Red Rock Review:* "Frida"; *Witness:* "The Red Horse"; *Writing Baseball* (Southern Illinois University Press): "Baseball"; and *3rd Bed:* "Diego."

ISBN 088739-476-0

Library of Congress Catalog Number 2002114939

Printed in the United States of America

TABLE OF CONTENTS

circling the tortilla dragon

PART ONE

HISTORICAL MARKER

On this site in 1532, Alonso Martinez de Salinas withdrew his sword from the saguaro and gasped at the stream of flying spiders that poured out of the tall, thick cactus. The spiders bounced off his steaming armor and Alonso stood there, hoping the current of awful things would stop emerging into the air. On this spot, he knelt and prayed for his wife and son whom he had not seen in twelve years, since his journey in search of gold and truth had taken him into the land of amputated people, groups of them asking him to give up his collection of their arms, feet, and legs. On this rock, in the same year, Alonso saw his first angel and proceeded to swing at it with his sword, his horse spooked by the fluttering wings, the rest of his men lost in the canyons for days. When he tired of stabbing at the night, Alonso paused at the edge of the cliff and watched a burning object cross the magnificent sky in seconds, its bright path realigning the desert stars so Alonso could carve his name and the name of his father on the red rock. On this site in 1956, a marble slab was erected by the state to give viewers the truth about conquest and the preserved alphabet of the lost, slashing lines of heavenly swords that cut the saguaro open each time a traveler stops and notices the dripping of sap on the ancient plant.

METAPHYSICAL LIGHT

They carried him to the top of the mountain where he could see his desert below as it changed into territory he could never own. The strong cities had burned long ago, the red cliffs transformed into doorways of fire that brought him answers he had spent a lifetime searching for, the origins of the questions hidden in war and conquest, and the official books that had kept his mind alive, but his legs wrong, had been rewritten. They carried him to a gentle place, laid him against a smooth rock near the last stream and let him gaze down on the history of the trails, the story of the pueblos, the movement of people he knew and those he never acknowledged, for the power he had accumulated had been used for the greater good of a handful of believers, the first ones to place their faith in a man who could not walk. They carried him to a place near the writings on the wall, prehistoric markings joined by names and dates from only four hundred years ago, some of the names familiar in his dreams, others carved there to add to the mysteries of his life and divert him from his final goal. He slept there and waited for energy from his years of wisdom and knowledge to return and heal him, the passage to the river now blocked by icebergs, previously unknown in the desert of eternal heat, the arrival of the ice pushing him to consolidate his holdings and take the boundaries of the ones he loved, extending them to the river that would never freeze, whose blue path would show him the way out of the troubled world. They carried him closer to the messages in the rocks and he loved it there, spending his days reading what others had written, learning the stories of people he had ignored, discovering three answers to questions that had haunted him for years—why did his father abandon him, why did the tall peaks of the Sangres de Dios attract the final lightning that hit the world, and why did the woman he loved disappear with the men of two heads that had invaded his riches and taken his prize? They moved him once or twice until he made his bed near an old kiva, his followers warning him this was not the best thing to do, not the ground to choose in a time when choices were limited. He defied them and slept there for five days—the dreams of golden trees, fountains of green water, and skies full of flying ships making him stronger, until he awoke one morning and turned to the wall to find every single pictograph, every ancient signature gone, the surface of the great wall as smooth and untouched as the back of the woman he had lost. They carried him down the mountain so he would stop weeping, letting him down in the soft, hot sand after he threatened them. They all stood back and were horrified when he stood on his own, his legs thin and wobbly, but holding him up, the one they had served most of their lives walking toward them, tracing a proud circle in the sand, showing them he had been right after all. They stood back because he had returned, their leader raising his arms to the sky and announcing they were free to go at last. A few ran away immediately, while others hesitated and gathered their things before leaving, two loyal followers staying with him because they knew someone had to carry him to the one place he had always wanted to go.

THE CRUCIFIX IS DOWN

The last crucifix is down off the wall, an outline of its cross standing out from the faded paint, the Christ having hung there for twenty-six years. The tenement apartment once contained fourteen such crucifixes, but the old woman has died at ninety-six and her family has taken them all away except for this one overlooked inside the closet. Three days after the apartment is cleared of the woman's belongings, the forgotten crucifix slips off the rusty nail and lands on the closet shelf, no one around to hear it fall, the thud on the wood announcing that it has landed with Christ's figure face up, its plunge off the wall forming a tiny dust cloud. The cross is eight inches long, the figure about six, its ivory-colored plastic cracked. Two more days go by before the apartment manager shows the place to a potential renter, the crucifix lying flat on the shelf and not seen when he opens the closet. He shows the apartment to four other possible tenants, but the place is not rented. Five days after the last inspection, the crucifix moves two inches closer to the edge. Three days later, painters are sent in because the manager thinks he can rent it after a painting of the ugly, turquoise walls. The closet doors are half open, so the two-man crew doesn't notice the bottom three inches of the cross, with Christ's feet and knees, teetering on the edge of the shelf. They paint the two main rooms in two days, saving the closet for last. One painter almost steps on the crucifix that is now lying, Christ down, on the floor. He calls to his partner, but the other painter is touching up in the bathroom. The discoverer picks up the crucifix and sets it on the kitchen counter where they have piled old nails, a twisted fly swatter, and other objects of a previous life. He paints the closet and notices the silhouette the crucifix left in the layers of grime that cover the rest of the wall. Before he paints that area, he stands back and observes the pale form left by the cross. He goes to the crucifix on the counter and finds it under old newspapers his partner found in the bathroom. Though he is not Catholic, he touches the cracked plastic Christ and is trying to recall something about his long dead father and priests, when a chilling cry scares him back. He drops the cross on the counter and runs into the bathroom. "What the hell?" he asks the other painter whose face is pale, the guy shaking in his splattered clothes. "I saw her," he says in a low voice, a brush with fresh paint dripping in his hand. The bathroom is empty, half the wall behind the tub painted yellow, the rest peeling its ugly pink. "I saw her sitting right there in the tub, covered in an Indian blanket. She was saying something like a prayer, then she held a Jesus up to me." Both men step out of the bathroom as this is described. The bathroom painter takes his baseball cap off and wipes the sweat with a painted hand. "She held one of those crosses up to me, then she was gone." He goes into the kitchen, and his partner follows, noticing the bleached outlines of other crosses on the bedroom and living room walls, places they have already painted over. He hears a rustling of newspapers and notices the rising strength of the paint fumes in the apartment. His partner, still shaking, is searching the crumbled newspapers for the crucifix. "I saw a cross right here earlier," he says. The two search the counter, but the crucifix is not there. Silently, they go to the closet and find the crucifix nailed to a spot that has already been painted, one nail at the top of the cross, one nail through the Christ's chest, and one nail through his crossed legs, the nails thicker and longer than the old ones they found the first day when they were preparing the walls—the heavy spikes shattering the plastic, while pinning the Christ deeper into the crucifix. No one remembers who ran out of the apartment first.

POETS DANCING TO A
FULL MOON

The poets dance to a full moon because they don't know what else to do with themselves. They are tired of fighting and competing, weary from writing and seeing things no one else can see. The poets dance to a full moon because they know it will never last, their words of wisdom and insight temporary and fragile, their books unread and filed away by a vicious reading public that doesn't even know they exist. The poets dance to a full moon when it comes close to the earth, their visions of invincibility followed by those of madness—meandering moonlight illuminating their ways of survival and taking their breath away at the end of each poem, at a public recital or at the peak of their powers. The poets dance to a full moon and the arrogant ball grows bigger, deeper than their most common phrases like "I love you, by the river, under the mountain, beyond the light." The poets dance to a full moon because its image controls their work—telling them when to rise and fall, when to love and hate, how to find the demon in the trees and how to pretend they have touched God. When one or two start to get tired, their cloaks drenched in sweat, the dance takes a turn, a detour, the highway signs toward the full thing in the sky knocked over when the poets can't find inspiration, the moment they dread when the cycle is a moonless sky that doesn't take names. The poets dance to a full moon when the world threatens to end and their families stop talking to them, old lovers they never cared about appearing at the door one day, contract in hand. Strangers and familiar faces thrust limited copies before their faces, asking for a signature, a sign—appraising one or two favorite poems the poet hates, the rare edition going up in price upon the appearance of the **X** on the page. The poets dance to a full moon when the only notion to strike is the will to write, the calling from a dark chamber that doesn't know the moon, the placement of one foot before the other in the study where drawers of notebooks turn yellow for tomorrow's archives, the future's hidden domain no one will break open before the earthquake takes the library away. The poets dance to a full moon when childhood returns and they must lecture the pain and the twisted moments away— fathers with leather belts, bullies with bloody knuckles, cold bedrooms in darkened houses with no one else around, the punishment for being who they are extending beyond midnight when no one comes home, unlocks the door or puts them to bed. The poets dance to a full moon because it is time to grieve, time to say and repeat, this hour of kissing and hugging, moments of temporary despair turning to bright flowers screaming across the heavens to pollenate the moon with tomorrow's reams of paper. The poets dance to a full moon because no one knows them and they don't know themselves after the publication of their first books. They dance and dance and continue to write, one or two loving each other, three or four hating the power around them, wondering what took them there and how often it struck, why it was so deep and shattering, the lasting light coming from a thriving world with no moon.

THE OLD MAN
WHO COMBED HIS HAIR

Roberto combed his long white hair each morning because the loose strands he caught in the wooden comb were signs from God. He read messages in the hair and grew wiser by what they said. The last time he collected a large ball of his hair, he sat down and studied the strands individually. The streaks of white told him the mountains above the village were going to change soon. The hair also revealed what happened to the lost children in the canyon—sons and daughters who had recently wandered into the desert and not returned. Roberto combed his hair and saw the children, some of them returning to the village from far away, others buried in fresh graves. He pulled the two longest strands from the ball of hair and gazed at the crooked white lines. Roberto found the face of a woman he once loved. He searched the house where he lived alone, but no one was there. The lantern glowed near the stove where he had cooked his dinner. He rose, set the ball of hair down, and gripped the two hairs in his left hand. He went to the wash basin at the other end of the room and squinted into the dirty mirror above the sink. Roberto smiled to himself because his hair kept growing, despite the baldness on top, and hung down over his shoulders. He heard a noise outside and went to the window. Parting the curtains, he saw a young boy and girl walk through his yard. The early evening darkness kept him from identifying who they were, which grieving family they came from. He opened the door and stepped onto his porch. The boy and girl, perhaps twelve or thirteen years old, paused near the cactus garden that grew along Roberto's fence, placed their hands on Roberto's gate and waited. Roberto ran one hand through his hair and sighed, the other still clutching the two hairs. No one moved until the shouts down the street caught their attention. The boy and girl greeted the four men and two women who appeared at Roberto's gate. One of the women sobbed and hugged her children. The men whispered among themselves and pointed to Roberto. They knew about his strange ways. They asked the boy and girl what had happened. They had been missing for three days. They asked if Roberto had anything to do with their disappearance. The girl shook her head in silence, but the boy told them he saw an old man in the canyon, though he wasn't sure if it was Roberto. Neither of the children had any idea why they crossed his yard on the way home or why they returned through this part of town. Roberto did not resist when the men entered his yard and grabbed him. They cursed and pushed him around, until one of them shouted to shave his head. Roberto tried to say something, but it was too late. They dragged him into his house, couldn't find any scissors, but grabbed a kitchen knife. Three of them held the old man down as a fourth cut his hair into ragged bunches. They kept cutting, until his head was nearly bald, stubby remains sticking out of his abused head. When they were done, they left in a hurry. Roberto lay on the floor for several hours. In the middle of the night, he rose and stumbled to the mirror. Without shock or pain, Roberto stared at himself. His head was covered in the longest, purest waves of white hair he had ever possessed. It hung to his waist and cascaded down his chest. This time, Roberto did not smile, but limped to his rocking chair. His neck was sore and bruised from the men, but he was covered in the purest white he had ever seen. He rocked slowly and held the ropes of hair in his open hands. Staring down at them, peaceful and content, Roberto could not see one moment of the world in the white fall of hair.

San Alfredo was the saint of sleep, blessing those who slept, protecting their faith in God from nightmares and dangerous daydreams. San Moro was the saint of long walks, guarding those who climbed ancient cliffs to dig for Indian artifacts, the trapped spirits in the walls of the pagans destroyed by Moro's flaming sword. San Bonifacio was the saint of caves, protecting the workers in the sulfur mines of Yuma, making the sign of the cross over the twenty-seven men who died in the 1923 explosion. San Moco was the saint of colds, waving his invisible cloak over the heads of the suffering, disappearing without a cure for those who fell asleep and had to turn to San Alfredo. San Peligroso was the saint of street corners where strangers hung out and questioned the faith of anyone who walked by, the cold medals of the saint they wore on their necks glistening in the night as each innocent person was questioned, threatened, and let go. San Vicente was the saint of bad art, taking his time blessing the alley fences and walls to make sure they were kept graffiti free. When a tagger from a different neighborhood invaded the alleys, it was San Vicente who scared him away by freezing the kid's can of spray paint. San Zolo was the saint of wild clothes, hiding in Goodwill stores to see if anyone would buy the Emilio Zapata t-shirt San Zolo craved, even if wearing it would defy the mightier God. When the pregnant mother couldn't find something to fit her for three dollars, San Zolo waved his arms and the tent flew from the camping department to the maternity rack, the expectant mother loving it for two dollars. San Copa was the saint of too much drinking, the smell he left behind noticeable by humans but never traced to the guardian who turned his back on wives who were beaten by drunk husbands, his power showing when the drunks did themselves in after years of agony from liver problems. San Frigoso was the saint of early sex, leering at the high school couple in the back seat, the cold air he created sending shivers over their naked bodies, until they dressed and drove away, his talent lying in his ability to make sure the condoms never broke, filtering out the ones with holes at the drugstore before the dudes could buy them. San Tripole was the saint of menudo, overseeing the cooking of great pots at busy restaurants, the posole and tripas the best medicine for people who didn't know the special flavor was made when San Tripole stuck both feet into the steaming pot right before the first bowl was served each morning. San Bolo was the saint of preserved rosaries, stepping into the territory of angels to guard old shoeboxes and trunks in cobwebbed attics and basements, where handfuls of old family rosaries were kept, some almost one hundred years old, hard beads and rusting chains tangling together, a rosary or two missing each decade as San Bolo reached in to pay back special favors to angels. San Grande was the saint of fat people, hating what San Tripole did to add to the problem, often lighting dark stairs or bathrooms as heavy bodies made their way there in the night, his duties beginning when the tonnage hit the floor and never moved, making sure relatives were around or emergency phone lines stayed open. San Logarto was the saint of lizards, fighting to keep hundreds of reptilian species alive despite the encroaching town, his talent at collecting lizard tails and dropping them into tiny matchboxes a gift the higher powers knew about and used during desert rainstorms when the tails were scattered through the black clouds and sent back to earth. San Mundo was the saint of the river, his skills called into question the year the entire town of faith was flooded, gravestones in the cemetery surviving the raging river that changed history when it yanked up each and every statue of these saints and washed them away forever, the surviving townspeople returning to San Antonio, San Martin, San Christopher, and San Jose.

THE TARANTULAS

Mario couldn't wake from his dream of the tarantulas. The closest one to his body was red and climbing closer. It approached his right arm which was extended down his side. Mario wanted to leap out of bed but was pinned down by an invisible force that allowed the tarantula to climb up his arm. In the final seconds of the dream, two more spiders were coming up his knees, their hairy legs tickling him. In the next dream, the tarantulas celebrated Mario's birthday. They were everywhere, some a deep black, others light brown. Every spider carried an upright birthday candle on its back. The fourteen flames lit the path for each tarantula that made its way around the chair where Mario sat. The tarantulas formed a circle around Mario, the bright candles waiting for him to sing Happy Birthday to himself before bending down to blow them out. The glow made the tarantulas seem larger. He squinted in the light of the dream and saw the tarantulas were growing. As each drop of wax fell on their backs, the heat made the spiders grow. Drip drip and the hairy things got bigger. Mario had had enough. He leaned forward in the uncomfortable chair, sucked in as much air as his lungs would hold and blew all the candles out, twisting his body to reach the candles behind him. All the flames went out and Mario woke up. He lay exhausted in his bed, his sweat-soaked t-shirt clinging to his heaving body. His breath slowed down and he blinked as he tried to get the vision of those tarantulas out of his head. In the early morning darkness, it took him a couple of minutes to notice the black tarantulas that clung perfectly still to the ceiling above his bed. An occasional twitch of a hairy leg told him he was not dreaming. He leaped out of bed before any of the creatures dropped on him. Gasping, he fell into the corner of the room, leaned against the cold wall and stared up at the spiders. He searched about wildly for a broom, overcome with fear and his urge to kill them. Then he noticed one of the spiders break away from the group and crawl across the ceiling by the window, and his fear diminished. It paused above the frame and waited. Mario tiptoed to the window, afraid he might scare it back into the room. He turned to check on the others, but the rest of the tarantulas were still directly above his bed. He carefully opened the window, the cool air from the morning making him stronger. As he expected, the lone spider moved down the glass and disappeared around the edge. He wanted to shut the window, but the motion on the ceiling took care of that. He went back to his corner as the careful parade of spiders made its way outside. He was fascinated, though relieved. Each black tarantula moved with a grace caught in the widening light of morning. Mario came closer as more of them went out the window. He could see the fine intricacy of the hair on their bodies, the way their repelling softness could also be attractive. As he drew closer, standing underneath the last three, he saw the hardened drops of wax on their bodies, his mother's favorite color, pink. The three spiders followed the others, and they were all gone. Mario went to his bed and studied the drops of pink wax frozen onto the white roughness of the ceiling. He wanted to run to his parent's room and tell them what had happened. Instead, he felt very tired and lay down. Without any more tarantulas to worry about, he quickly fell asleep, the window open to the outside, the patterns formed by the frozen drops of wax on the ceiling leading him to the next dream.

PYRAMID

I come out of the jungle and find the massive pyramid overgrown with vines. I have been searching for it for years, wasted several research grants traveling the Americas to find it, and here it is at last. I wipe sweat from my forehead with my hankie and behold its ancient brilliance. Most of the stairs have been worn down over the centuries and I don't think I can climb to the top. There are several strange markings on one wall. As a scholar of lost civilizations, I am familiar with many forgotten languages, but these petroglyphs are unknown to me. I am totally baffled by the way certain animals have been drawn around unusual letters and symbols. In one, what appears to be a crocodile is being prayed to by five kneeling men. In another, large flying birds are holding bows and flinging arrows at running stick men. As I peer at these images through my sunglasses, a purple snake crawls toward the wall about ten feet away. I turn to make sure no more reptiles are at my feet, but don't see any. Within seconds, the purple snake has disappeared into a crack in the wall. I hike around the pyramid and plan my course of action. I climb over fallen chunks of stone and trip over vines, but make it all the way around to where I began, convinced this is the place to conduct my studies. I stop near the crack where the snake entered, and pull a can of spray paint from my knapsack. I draw bright orange letters on the pyramid. "Steve does it with Mary" on one wall. A couple of feet above that—"Wanna a good time? Call Fernie's mother" and I write her phone number in the day glow orange. I work for almost an hour, the remote corner of the jungle leaving me alone to pronounce things like "Jito Gives Blow Jobs." "Rosaldo was here," even "Gringo Go

Home." Then I run out of paint, and I don't want to open another can. I step back and marvel at what I have done, pleased that I have not damaged a single ancient marking with the paint. Now, all I have to do is wait for my theories to be proven. I retreat into the jungle, pause to make notes in my journal about how the purple snake may complicate things, then head to the canoe. When I reach the boat, the silent Talo, my Mayan guide, listens as I tell him that this has been a very successful expedition.

LACQUERED SHOES

The pair of tiny shoes lacquered in copper belonged to a baby who hadn't made it, their miniature feet lasting less than two weeks before the baby died and the family placed the shoes on the mantle as a reminder. Dust gathered inside the shoes, the copper slowly turning darker, their wooden base cracking and peeling over the decades as they were joined by objects like a family photograph, a statue of an Aztec warrior, and a fossil stone from the river. One summer, when the family was away for several weeks, a tiny white spider found its way into one shoe, the layer of fine dust offering the perfect foundation for the strongest web the white spider ever built. A rush of air into the room had allowed the spider to float across the fireplace and land in the shoe, but this rare current of air in the closed house did not reappear when the spider wanted out and couldn't climb the smooth cliffs of copper. It died because no insect or natural prey entered the baby's shoes. The spider turned into a delicate pattern of white, and then the next breath of air two months later lifted it invisibly and sent it into the curtain by the window. This new disturbance originated with the person who broke into the house, stole the few antiques that could be carried, then fled. The intruder left fingerprints on the mantle and pushed dust against the shoes that were never touched, the lines of dirt traced by the intruder's fingers attracting a large moth that found its way into the room through the shattered window. It fluttered blindly against the wall, then landed on the rim of one of the lacquered shoes. It perched there, folded its wings over the shoe and died. When the family returned three weeks later, they reported the burglary and the police came and made a list of stolen objects, but no one noticed the gray moth on the mantle. The mother of the baby cleaned up the broken glass, pausing by the

RAY GONZALEZ

mantel when the lacquered shoes made her think of her child, holding her breath when she spotted the strange thing covering one of the shoes. By this time, the moth resembled a flat piece of paper and the patterns on its wings looked like the handwriting of a child. The woman gasped when she realized what this was, what it meant. She used a pair of tweezers to lift the note off the shoes and set it on an empty page of the family photograph album she kept. She sat on the sofa by the mantel and studied the note, convinced that it was a sign from her baby. The note read, "Mommy, I love you. Where are my shoes?" The woman cried silently, her husband away on business. For an instant, she thought she heard his voice, then the cry of her baby. She rose quickly and went to the mantel. She had to stand on tiptoe to look inside the dusty copper shoes. She realized she hadn't polished the shoes since her baby died. She peered inside each and was met by the remains of an old spider web in one, and half an inch of fine, gray powder in both. As she wept, the transparent remains of the moth flew off the open page of the scrapbook on the coffee table and landed on the carpet, a breeze from the kitchen doorway pushing them under an antique bookcase without a sound. The woman opened her eyes, wiped her nose on her sleeve, and turned to her prized photo album. She gasped at the empty page, her child's note gone, the yellow sheet waving in the morning light. She sat down on the sofa and leafed through the album, but the note was gone. "No! No!" she screamed and pounded the sofa with a fist. Throwing the scrapbook on the floor and not caring that some of the photos fell out, she went to the mantel and took the lacquered shoes in her arms for the first time in many years.

circling the tortilla dragon

PART TWO

ZAPATISTA DOLLS

Juan Felipe de Tierra went to the Mexican art exhibit at the Chicano Museum of Art in San Francisco and saw the Zapatista dolls there, four of them mounted in a fighting stance as part of a larger presentation on political events in Mexico. The dolls were the size of Barbies and were dressed in camouflage clothes with ski masks over their faces, tiny M16 rifles in their plastic arms. Juan Felipe stood among the visitors and couldn't believe that the guerrilla movement from Chiapas had been transformed into dolls. Reading the sign near the three male and one female doll, he found they were made by a Chicano artist, not the Zapatistas themselves. He wandered around the galleries and entered the gift shop where two dolls stood on a shelf, price tag of $26.00 hanging on each black mask. The young Chicana behind the counter smiled at him. "Aren't they cool?" she asked after dropping three Virgen de Guadalupe postcards into a bag for another shopper. "Who gets the money for the dolls?" Juan Felipe asked. "Pato Jimenez the artist was donating twenty dollars to the Zapatistas for each doll. We already sold two and have two left," she explained. Juan Felipe shook his head at her answer and walked out. He enjoyed the Mexican exhibit himself, but wondered how many Chicanos really identified with Mexico. Most of his students seemed too wrapped up in their U.S. self-absorption. After stopping for coffee, Juan Felipe crossed through the parking lot where he had left his car. Two vehicles away, he spotted a Zapatista doll on the ground, its rifle missing and both arms extended above its head like a football referee signaling a touchdown. Juan Felipe picked it up and examined it. Under the camouflaged Army pants and tight ski-mask, he found a plastic doll like the Ken doll a student had once brought to class as part of a presentation on Barbie and Ken and their impact on American poetry. Juan Felipe pulled the mask off and a pale, blue-eyed Ken smiled at him. $26.00 for this? He wondered who Pato Jimenez was. He was gripping the guerrilla in one hand and reaching for his keys with the other, when a shrill whistle scared the shit out of him and car tires screeched all around. Before Juan Felipe knew anything, five men in suits with guns drawn had jumped out of three vehicles and were screaming,"Get your hands up! Get your hands up!" Juan Felipe dropped the Zapatista doll as one of the men slammed him into his car hood. His glasses flew off as the man savagely hand-cuffed him and spun him around. "Who the fuck are you?" the suit hissed through his Right Guard deodorant smell. "What the fuck are you doing?" he added. Juan Felipe couldn't speak as two more men in sunglasses surrounded him. "This is my car," Juan Felipe managed to say as he coughed. "I just found the doll." "Shut up!" one of them yelled as his boss stepped in. The fourth man stared at Juan Felipe through tiny shades. "Let him go. It's not him," he pronounced. The others dashed to their cars as the one who had hand-cuffed him unlocked him. "Big mistake," the boss told Juan and motioned to the other man. They rushed to their vehicles and the three cars sped away. Juan Felipe fell against his car, wanting to throw up. He stared at the Zapatista doll at his feet. He kicked it and its arms flew up again as it landed a few feet away. He caught his breath, then he picked up the doll. Feeling dizzy, he ran across the street, dodging several passing cars as he burst into the museum shop. It was empty and he startled the girl behind the counter. "Did you see what just happened?" he yelled at her. The girl's dark eyes widened. "What?" she asked when she saw the doll in his shaking hands. "I found this in the lot over there and got attacked by some men!" Juan Felipe spat at her. "Did you sell this today?" She took it from him and studied the Zapatista doll. "We sold them all today," she said, "but I've never seen this one before. This isn't one of Pato's dolls." Juan Felipe turned to find the empty shelf that had held the two dolls he saw earlier. "Did men in suits buy them after I left?" he asked the girl, who was getting nervous. She shrugged. "Where did you get this one?" she said. "It isn't one of Pato's." Juan grabbed it from her. "How do you know that?" The girl searched for the other clerk. With watery eyes, she looked at Juan. "All of Pato's dolls have brown skin and they do not have blue eyes. A Chicano man dressed like you and me bought the last two a few minutes ago. Don't you know?" Juan Felipe tried to stay calm, "Know what?" The girl breathed easier when an older Chicana woman appeared from the storeroom. "Pato Jimenez died two months ago," the second clerk explained. "He was shot and killed in Chiapas by Mexican soldiers who attacked the town where he went to deliver medical supplies to the Zapatistas." Juan stared at the women and gripped his doll tighter. He didn't know what to say, so he ran out of the shop in search of the man who had bought the other dolls. Juan Felipe searched up and down the busy San Francisco street, but found no one. Giving up, he threw the blue eyed Zapatista in the dumpster by the parking lot, keeping a wary eye out for the suits as he headed back to his car.

THE MURAL OF
BABY LIZARD

Henry "Baby Lizard" Martinez was the leader of the homeboys and an artist. He got his nickname from swallowing a tiny lizard on a dare when he was five years old. At sixteen, he was chosen to do a mural for the city project to save the vatos from their neighborhood violence. The city supplied the paint and chose the wall. Baby Lizard's mural still stands on the abandoned building at the corner of Piedras and Pershing streets. The painting is of two happy low riders on top of two huge, balloon-shaped cars with green and red fenders shining above black tires the size of the world. The grinning vatos wore their hair like the richest lords of El Paso, and Baby Lizard's technique blew them up to the size of cigarette dudes, like the Marlboro Man on the billboard across the street. A few bullet holes have added their mark to the mural, but Baby Lizard is not around to touch it up. He became a famous artist in prison, sold many paintings for bread he sent back to Juana and his sisters, was stabbed years ago by his cellmate who didn't like the size of the lips Baby Lizard drew on a caricature of him. The low riders on the mural are famous. The city had a contest and the winning names were Prieto and Lalo the Duck. The building was saved by a neighborhood group, Baby Lizard carrying the newspaper article about it in his back pocket until the day he died. The mural of Baby Lizard keeps getting larger. It is initiation for the new homeboys. They must climb the wall and carve their initials in the enormous sunglasses of Prieto and Lalo, who ride their '56 Chevy into the sunset each evening, grinning down at every drive-by whose passengers are no longer the darkest things on the streets.

CORKY MENDOZA

Corky Mendoza returns from the dead to haunt the boys who shot him. He appears in their dreams, their jail cells, in their parents' beds, and between the legs of their girlfriends. Corky is everywhere, the way he died framed in the history of the barrio, another drive-by dancer off to see where his ancestors inhabited the great territory of tenement houses torn down on Guadalupe street forty years ago. When he burst through the tunnel of light, he saw Anselmo, Corrina, Pedro, Dionisio, and Joaquin. They were all knifed to death before Corky was born. He joins them in the flying chamber of walls and clouds, where he learns the Spanish of the galaxy, the brittle curse words of the comet, so he can return to the streets and sing to the homeboys who score. Corky comes back from the dead and places two cold barrels of light against the heads of the six vatos who did it, locks his tattooed arms around their necks so they can dream of each other and have visions of flowers. Rows of landscaped names brandish the sun with the green walk of mourners, shooters, rappers, and Catholic head-shaved boys tracked down by Corky night after night, drive-by after drive-by, until the legend of Corky is larger than the bleeding colors on the murals peeling off the bullet-riddled walls of the house where Corky was born.

THE LATER LIFE OF
MONCHITO

In the later life of Monchito, he peeled oranges and ate slices that revealed green butterflies sleeping in the wrong fruit. In the later years of his knowledge, he made love to three women under a portrait of a woman with her orange hair on fire, the violin on her left shoulder smoldering with Monchito's habit of leaving before morning. In the later perceptions of his age, a new guest arrived in his journals and influenced what Monchito recalled about the flooded city of his birth. In later attempts at survival, he opened the door of his apartment to a woman he didn't know, her arms holding a bag of oranges, her white dress covered in prints of green butterflies. In the later years of his silence, Monchito forgot this woman and moved into the fields to dig potatoes. He worked there for several seasons, his back burning with the weight of what he had never done before. In the later return to his border, Monchito found a box under his bed containing three guitar picks, four rubber bands, one three-inch rubber dildo, six pencils branded with Josie's Tire Shop on them, a slipcover for a rare Beatles 45 rpm vinyl record, two packages of charcoal drawing sticks, one Valentine card with pictures of Vishnu and Shiva on the front, and fourteen clean popsicle sticks. In the last will of Monchito, he insisted that these items be returned to their unknown owners and left twenty-three journals of his writing, three pairs of worn shoes, four old pairs of pants, no underwear, and not one single writing instrument. On closer inspection, the six pencils were actually erasers. In the later life of Monchito, nobody came forward to claim these items.

THE BULLFIGHT

Antonio dodges the swipe of the bull's horns and feels hot air swish by his chest, and the enormous creature makes the ground tremble. The red cape swims in the humid air like a flag of blood, but it is too early for such things. Antonio glances down at the dirt and loves the outfit he has chosen today, its blue and gold leggings perfect for the largest crowd in the ring this season. He runs out of time to think when the bull turns and charges again, even before he can taunt it. He holds his ground as the bull flings the cape out of its way and misses stepping on his foot by inches. Antonio doesn't like the chunks of dirt that fly into his face and land on his beautiful vest. It tells him this bull is alert and playing games with the matador, the deafening roar of the crowd making him focus as the first beads of sweat pour down his face. The bull continues the dance, not slowing down even when Antonio jabs three colorful, short lances into its back. The blood runs around Antonio's feet, and this goes on and on, sweat completely soaking the matador, the bull not giving an inch in the mire of red dirt. Antonio is handed the sword for the final kill and waits for the bull which has stopped twenty yards from him, its huge nostrils steaming blood into the afternoon air. It comes on and finds Antonio in its rage. The matador plunges the sword two seconds before the bull enters him, splitting his ribcage, throwing him into the air. Antonio finds the shoulders of the bull high off the ground, black muscle shining beneath the colorful streamers and flags the crowd has thrown into the ring. Antonio thinks of Maria, his wife, how she draped a black silk shawl over her naked breasts the night before, and the sky of love and power turns a brighter blue at the moment of impact with the bull. Antonio blinks his eyes in a field of dandelions, the fence on his father's ranch the first detail he recognizes, the smoke of its burning houses rising in the distance as the bloody mud of triumph sings through his legs when he spots the approaching cavalry of invaders. Their glistening bandoliers, rifles, and horses give way to the bull as it drops and dies, Antonio's red cape waving across the stadium full of shocked, silent people.

THE SURREALIST PAINTER

Flaco Aragon was one of the greatest Surrealist painters of his time, the visions and chaos on his canvases changing the world of art in his country, but by the age of fifty-four, the manic speed with which he painted was starting to catch up with him. He slept in his messy studio, cans of paint and fumes from thinner intoxicating him twenty-four hours a day. Flaco had sold five paintings in the past month, museum curators paying him twelve thousand dollars, his reputation allowing him to call his own shots without anyone representing him on the market. One night, the huge brown head with three smaller heads in each eye and mouth came to him. He painted it and sold it for three thousand dollars within days. Later that week, the dismembered woman with burning pigeons flying out of her breasts appeared in a dream and he worked all night, calling a dealer from his waiting list and selling it for six thousand dollars. The third painting in days of exhaustion and madness consisted of the tiny head of his estranged daughter Alicia wrapped in olive leaves and held in the lap of a winged monster, its sunglasses and baseball cap appearing in Flaco's work for the first time. The monster, green and blue with candy canes protruding out of its ears, held Alicia's head in its lap and mocked Flaco as he stood wearily by the canvas. This enraged the artist, so he painted a vulva on what was supposed to be a male monster. The alien stared at him through its shades, so Flaco painted a penis to replace one of the candy canes. By the light of morning, Flaco finished his latest painting by drawing a smile on his daughter's kind face. This hurt, but he knew it was the final touch. He slept for two days before calling another dealer who promised five thousand dollars without seeing the painting. When a Mr. Dover appeared at his studio door the following morning, Flaco opened it wearing nothing but a rainbow jockstrap, a momento he owned from his affair with Peggy Cisneros, a notorious prima donna writer and collector of Latin American men and their art. Mr. Dover, a short, balding man with thick eyeglasses, stared at the jockstrap the entire time he spent with Flaco. The painter limped to the canvas, flipped the protective cover off, and watched as Mr. Dover almost had an orgasm over his new masterpiece. The little man wrote a check on the spot, covered the painting again and tried to carry it out, though it was larger than he. Flaco put on a pair of pants and helped the museum wank carry the painting to his van downstairs. Mr. Dover thanked him and drove away. When Flaco returned to his fume-filled studio, a fresh canvas he didn't recall mounting sat on his favorite easel, Alicia's head in charcoal the lone object drawn on it. Flaco stared at it because he never used charcoal. Did Mr. Dover do this when Flaco was getting dressed? The Surrealist actually felt tranquil with the image of his daughter on the white canvas. Though he had not spoken to her in eight years, her image could be traced in several of his greatest pieces—but how did this one show up? Flaco heard a noise behind him and turned as Mr. Dover let himself in, the tiny man naked except for a rainbow jockstrap of his own, this one about to burst with the museum man's erection. Flaco was about to throw him out and call his boss when Mr. Dover pulled a check out of his jock-strap and showed Flaco the ten thousand dollar figure. Flaco motioned to Mr. Dover to sit on his paint covered sofa. The horrible little man with the enormous pointer lay on the couch with a smile and waited as Flaco shut the door. The painter went to a table and opened two cans of paint. Before the representative of the art world could say anything, the Surrealist spilled baby blue and yellow paint on him, the drops stinging the little man's eyes, making him sit up and gag. Flaco grabbed the white hairs on his hairy chest, heard the man scream, and tossed him against the canvas with his daughter's head. The blue and yellow streaks formed beautiful patterns but did not touch Alicia's image. Mr. Dover tried to rub the paint out of his stinging eyes, but Flaco opened the door and kicked his ass down the stairs. The naked Mr. Dover must have crawled to his waiting van because Flaco never saw him again. He worked for three days straight to finish one of his greatest paintings, which he sold to another museum for twelve thousand five hundred dollars. The painting, titled "Colors of Love," is on the cover of Flaco Aragon's best-selling monograph, "Rainbow Distrust: The Art of Flaco Aragon." Two years after the creation of "Colors of Love" and its exhibition at a Surrealist Show in Paris, Flaco Aragon was found dead in his studio by a fellow Surrealist painter, Mundo Parrot, who told police there was blue and yellow paint smeared on Flaco's frozen lips when he found his friend.

MY LIFE AS A LIZARD

I was a proud lizard, tiny and quick, boys with BB guns shooting at me often but always missing. The summer the tarantulas invaded the desert, I was one of the few lizards that stood his ground, protecting my rocks with sudden movements that led the spiders to nest in other holes. My life as a lizard was also a search for water—raindrops huge as entire worlds falling so rarely that when they did, I would collect them on my back and spread them around, sharing them with the collar lizard and the chuckwalla, slapping each raindrop off my scales with my quick tail, the water landing wherever the other lizards desired. The year of the great dust storm gave me new powers, the tunnels I cleared through the rising sand leading the lizards to higher ground, though several dozen of us disappeared and were never seen again. My life as a lizard made me challenge the diamond back rattler that entered the arroyo one night, its long, sleek body taking over the weeds, its mute presence waiting for something to happen, for one of us to make the first move. When I darted from under the rocks and it struck, the missiled fangs cut off my tail and sent me flying bare-assed, throwing me over the cliff and into a world I had never seen before. I lay stunned on a hard surface, distant lights getting closer, their enormous suns growing brighter as they approached, the massive wind that surrounded their beams throwing me farther down the shoulder of the road as they passed. My life as a lizard was a dream of a hot land, followed by the cool calmness of glass, the enormous letters on its surface staying there, day and night, my origins explained and spelled out for endless faces of monsters like none I had ever seen before, some of them laughing in wonder at my confinement, how I hid under the stone turtle, or climbed the plastic tree that never grew. One thing that was different was now there was constant water in the dish, my tail growing back in no time, bright suns pointing at me for hours before going out, then pointing again in a cycle I got used to—noises outside the glass coming and going, the monsters dropping grasshoppers and flies among my two rocks every day, this gift changing the way I grew, the method by which I came to understand. One dark time, during a period of no sun, I heard a sudden noise and thought the rattler was back. I slid into the thin layer of sand as the glass broke, the tree and water flying away from me as a monster pushed everything away and scratched huge symbols on the walls before running away like all of us he released—sudden flight I had not known in a long time, my new tail and rested legs sending me across a cold surface that led to dozens of other lizards, tarantulas, and even a scorpion running across the river of glass pointing to a wide open door. As we scattered in every direction, I did not have to be told where I was or wait for lizards from my old nest to guide me home. I found the way back, my freedom a dirt trail to a desert I had breathed before because I crossed an arroyo like the one from home. I had to thread my way through dozens, even hundreds of lizard and turtle bones, tiny filaments and skeletons from recent failures, mounds of them becoming dirt and dust, intimate grains from the life as a lizard I had always known.

circling the tortilla dragon

PART THREE

I WILL GIVE YOU
A GREAT MYTH

A cricket chirps one morning, hoping its young will return from the crushed sidewalk. On this rainy day, the cricket risks the running water and emerges from the grass. It is swept down the concrete toward a river on the edge of town. It manages to land on a rock before it can be swept into the current, stopping close to two naked men who are building a fire in the woods along the bank. The men keep trying to build a fire in the wet air, their bodies bristling with rain. The cricket watches them, then chirps on the rock a few yards away. When one of them notices the sound of a cricket, he looks about the camp wildly, his bare torso bouncing huge raindrops. He can't find the chirping thing, but the fire is lighted by the other man as he searches. When they huddle around the fire, the cricket leaps closer. When it chirps again, the man with the larger penis reaches behind him and grabs the cricket with his eyes closed. As he squeezes, the wet thing pops out of his fingers and disappears in the rising flames. The two men huddle closer, water dripping down their thick folded legs, the hunger in their bellies moving as each dreams about the taste of cricket, a sustenance they keep within, because neither knows how to tell the other that one of them is going to take the blame.

circling the tortilla dragon

KOMODO DRAGON

There is a Komodo dragon in my backyard. It has my cat in its mouth and chews it savagely as I appear on the porch. The Komodo is at least twelve feet long and larger than an alligator. When it swallows the cat, a cloud of hairs hangs in the air in front of its mighty face. The Komodo tramples through my mother's flowers and stops under our small willow tree. It looks up at the birdcage my mother hung on the willow for decoration. There are no birds in it, but the Komodo raises itself on its back legs and rips the wooden cage off the tree. The sound of snapping, crunching wood punctuates the morning. I come out of my shock and reach for the garden hose coiled on the porch. I don't know what else to do, so I turn it on full and spray the Komodo with a jet of water. It is twenty yards from me, but the water seems to work because it stops, its huge feet slowly sinking in the mud, the water ricocheting off its body. It closes its eyes and doesn't move because I think it loves the water! I stand there for minutes, spraying it and flooding the backyard. I want to drop the hose and run inside to call 911, but all I can do is wet this content creature. The Komodo has sunk low enough in the mud to swim. I keep the powerful jet of water on its head as I flood the yard. The head seems to be the spot, but I have to really aim because the Komodo is floating away on the lake that has rapidly formed. It keeps its eyes shut as the water carries it across the yard, our flowers and nicely trimmed grass now a swamp. I grab the hose head with both hands because my wrist is getting sore, but I can't stop because this is working. The Komodo is a hypnotized mountain of muscle sailing toward the twisted and torn back gate where it entered, and I hope it doesn't get caught in the metal. I descend the stairs with the hose, my nozzle pointing the way. The Komodo is asleep as it makes it through the gate, but the hose doesn't reach any farther. What do I do if it wakes up? The Komodo has come to a halt in the middle of the alley, which is dry. I can't reach its head with the hose any longer, so I drop it and run. Before I reach the porch stairs, a screech of tires and the sounds of a heavy engine reverberate in the alley. I remember that today is trash day. The crew calmly get out of the truck and two guys with gloves lift the sleeping dragon by its head and tail, swing it a couple of times, then toss it high into the compactor. I yell, "Wait! Wait! That's a Komodo dragon!" The roar of the compactor drowns me out as they climb in and drive down the alley. I run to the gate as the truck halts by the street. It shakes and explodes and the compactor flies into pieces as this enormous Godzilla monster rises from the back, its enormous jaws foaming with crushed soda cans, styrofoam, and plastic bags full of my neighbor's trash. I run as the horrifying screams of the garbage crew echo down the alley.

I was walking down the street with my friend Emilio after dinner at his mother's house, when suddenly a huge prickly pear cactus started growing rapidly out of his head. He screamed and held his head with both hands as the sharp thorns and green flesh of the cactus emerged through the top of his skull, hair and bone splitting apart as the prickly pear shot toward the sky. Emilio closed his eyes and the cactus stopped growing, three feet of the twisted plant sticking heavily out of his head, five or six thorny arms bending in all directions, their weight making Emilio bend forward as if he was about to fall. I rushed to him and tried to hold him up, though the thorns protruding toward me made it difficult to reach him. I didn't know what to say because Emilio was now on his knees, the heavy cactus pushing him down until he was sitting on the ground. That's when I noticed the first three or four birds, circling low over us and then landing in a tall oak behind a brick wall. Emilio steadied himself with both hands, but couldn't speak, his eyes shut in a tight grimace, his mouth wide open in an O of shock and humiliation. I didn't know what to do, the two of us alone on the quiet street of the evening, a few people crossing at the corner without spotting the man with the prickly pear mass sticking out of his head and his helpless friend standing there staring at the bright green thing and noticing the moist odor it gave off. Emilio shifted to his knees as the cactus gave one last heave and another foot of the plant pushed out of his head, the sharp skin on this final section containing what looked like pieces of Emilio's brain. At that moment, I started to panic, but still couldn't speak or ask Emilio what we should do. Emilio balanced himself and tried to stand. I moved to help him, but was blocked by the flutter of wings as seven or eight sparrows landed on Emilio's cactus, the thorns not keeping them from finding places to roost. They began a chorus of chirping and singing, the notes rising above my suffering friend, a couple of sparrows shitting on what remained of Emilio's hair as they sang. He staggered forward and signaled for us to keep going. I wanted to help him, but the cactus and its sparrows seemed to propel Emilio forward. I walked beside him, staying a few feet back from the pointed barbs and watching the sparrows jump from one cactus arm to another. We managed to reach the corner, not another soul in sight, Emilio's face slowly turning purple with the weight of the prickly pear and birds on his mind. He managed to open his eyes halfway and his mouth didn't seem as wide, the sweat pouring down his pained face. Two birds darted away and a few more sparrows followed as we stopped. I clearly recall three birds left on the arms of the cactus in Emilio's head when Maria, Emilio's mother, screeched to a halt in her old Mustang Ford. The three sparrows stopped chirping at once, on one note, as she swerved onto the sidewalk, the car churning asphalt and grass, almost hitting us. I jumped back, but the cactus kept Emilio rooted where he stood. I heard Emilio moan with his eyes closed again, as if the sight of his mother finding him like this was the last straw, the final cry. Maria, a very overweight woman who had divorced Emilio's father when her son was twelve, struggled out of her rusty car, reached into her purse and pulled out a metal can of gasoline and the biggest box of wood matches I had ever seen. Before I could stop her, she poured gasoline on her son and his cactus, then flicked a match across the box. The flame jumped in the night air as Maria's gasoline lit the cactus on her son's head, though the thick arms were green and I didn't think they would burn. What I still recall is those three sparrows just sitting there as if hypnotized among the thorns, the fire crackling and spreading on Emilio's head, the smoke and flames consuming the sparrows that never moved. Maria leaned on her car as her son's prickly pear exploded into a giant ball. She screamed in the night as the smoke descended over her son's head, covering him completely, his body becoming a gruesome torch. I turned to Maria as she screamed at her son, "I told you not to eat so many vegetables! I told you not to eat so many vegetables!" Her pronouncement finally made me speak. "We didn't! You gave us a great meal at your house but there were no vegetables! Menudo and tortillas are not vegetables." As Emilio turned to ashes, his mother shed her first tears. In the distance, I could hear sirens. "I raised him on too many nopales, cactus greens from my garden," she ended in a whisper as we stared at the last smoke that used to be Emilio, the cactus scorched to nothing, the birds that stayed on the thorns now tiny pieces of charcoal on the ground.

JUAREZ BEES

They swarm in the tower of the church of La Virgen de Guadalupe, then fly out of the belfry in a black cloud of miracles. The Tarahumara Indian woman with no legs looks up from her wooden platform on wheels, the sky turning the color of her hair. The Juarez bees can't find the border, can't escape the savage humming of heat when the captured young men float dead on the Rio Grande. The Tarahumara woman in the plaza searches the air for the bees, the humming transformed into the stumps that used to be her knees, until she feels her feet have returned after being crushed for forty-two years. She looks down, but her dirty, torn skirt covers what is left. She knows her feet. A hairful of bees descends into the crowded streets, people running and screaming as the bees flash in lines of blue and electric wind, the rest of the swarm following the river for a few miles, then turning back toward the church. The Juarez bees reenter the church in the evening, the red light of the setting sun igniting the air with sounds the Tarahumara remembers from her days as a little girl who used to stick her hands into the rich honeycombs of San Luis Potosi, her dripping fingers blessing her face with the sweetness of honey and a body of honey no one could break. The church is locked that night, the bees settle in the bricks, and the old woman rolls down the sidewalk among the people strolling in the darkness, their dropped coins already sparkling in the street.

Frida paints another portrait of Diego, but this time gives him two heads and a pair of wings, and makes his body very thin. No one will recognize the great bleeding artist in her painting. Frida works for several days, the detailed piece showing Diego as he hovers over a strange woman's bed, the angry faces on his two heads arguing with one another, perhaps trying to decide which head gets to go down between the woman's legs first. Frida does this to Diego for several days, until the painting is finished. She reaches for her cane, limps a few feet away from the piece, then turns to study it. It is exactly what has come in her dreams for a long time. Diego is out of the country again, but she can wait until he returns to show him what she has created. She spends the next few days painting two pieces she is not quite happy with, neither having anything to do with her husband. The one that surprises her with its need for so much red paint is of a small heart within a larger heart. In the middle of the smaller one hangs a birdcage, the contraption floating in the red muscle like the medallion of a turtle Frida wears around her neck. One week after finishing the two-headed Diego, Frida rises in the cool morning and makes coffee, then goes to the window of her quiet studio and moves the curtains aside. Sparrows clatter in the birdbath she has in the patio, but there is something different this morning. The cactus plant she had growing in a heavy pot on the ground has been dumped into the birdbath. She goes outside to clean up the mess, wondering why anyone would do such a thing. The pot is not broken, but the dark soil has muddied the bird's water. Despite the cactus plant floating in the shallow bath, she has to shoo a couple of birds out of the water. She pricks one finger when she grabs the cactus and dumps it in the pot. As she licks her finger and tastes blood, she also tastes the rich soil in the pot and thinks of Diego. She sets the heavy planter on the ground, bends down to grab a mound of soil that fell around it, and notices the drawing on the side of the pot. Someone has taken blue and yellow chalk and painted two hearts there, blue hearts outlined with bright yellow. She drops the dirt and holds up the planter in the morning light. Has Diego returned to her? No. He would never play these kinds of games. She stares at the two hearts, the anger in their marriage making her throw the pot hard to the ground where it breaks into shards. She hurries into her studio where the heart within the heart beats on her easel. Taking blue and yellow paint from her work table, she forms a third heart right over the red ones, covers the birdcage with the new paint, heart upon heart dripping into each other. Her pricked finger is now covered with paint, the doors and windows of her studio thrown open to the sharp light of morning, the chirping of sparrows reminding her of the painting of a two-headed Diego she is going to destroy when she is done tearing the hearts to shreds.

COLLECTING PARROTS

He collected parrots—live ones (he had seven), dead ones stuffed and mounted, on postcards, in photos, even illustrations of parrots on his t-shirts. He lived and breathed parrots. The odd thing is he never named his parrots, though he knew them by sight, habits, and swore each had a different voice. He taught them different words and was amazed at the few similar words they each repeated. It was as if each had to keep its own identity and not copy others. "Give me a coke." "Tortilla! Tortilla" "Harry's home! Harry's home!" "Cabrón!" "Answer the door." Even "ABC! ABC!" This was a list of the favorite phrases by his seven nameless parrots. He lived in a mountain of blue, yellow, green, white, and red feathers and, of course, dwelled in a river of parrot shit and smell. The curtains in his living room had parrot patterns on them and the community of cages and perches dominated that part of his house. He worked at home as a computer geek and had built a successful business in selling parrot paraphernalia over the internet. His two garages were full of parrot coffee cups, pillows with parrots, stuffed parrot toys, parrot decals, key chains with plastic parrots tied on them, white clay statues of parrots ready to be painted, even table mats with parrots—everything parrot, and he made several thousand dollars a month from customers all over the country. Things were going well, even though he was too busy for a love life, until one day, two of his parrots fell dead off their perches. He walked into the room and discovered them, the other five parrots perched as if nothing had happened. They started talking to him in their usual manner, ignoring the two stiff birds on the carpet. He ran to them in a panic, not knowing what had happened. The parrots would fight occasionally, but nothing serious. He picked up the dead birds and carried them out of the room. The other five stopped talking at once, on one note. He gently laid the dead parrots in a box he was going to use for shipping an order. He was surprised at not feeling deep sadness when he covered them with newspaper, put the lid on the box, and took it to the garbage can outside the kitchen door. He dropped them in there without a second look. When he came back inside, he heard the new words streaming from the community room—"Kill him! Kill him!" "Lets go! Lets go!" "Watch the door! Watch the door!" "There he is! There he is!" He was stunned because he had never taught his pets these awful phrases. The surviving five parrots were repeating them in unison, the squawking choir rising in pitch and fury. He ran into the room to find the five of them flying around awkwardly, flapping into each other, knocking perches to the floor, all five switching places and landing in new spots around the room. "Kill him! Watch the door!" This loud command came from his favorite bird—the largest and oldest parrot he owned, whose proud blue and green feathers seemed to point at him as it flapped its wings. Its betrayal made him lunge toward its perch, but it sprang into the air and his outstretched arms hit the window instead. He cried out in pain, which scared all five parrots. They flew out of the room in one swoop, five heavy birds maneuvering down the hallway. He raced after them, remembering that their chatter had made him leave the kitchen door open, something he had never worried about before. When he reached the kitchen, three of them were already gone, the two youngest parrots hesitating on the table, almost calm. He slammed the door shut and was able to pet the two of them gently and carry them back to the community room. It took several days to recover and get back to the computer. He never found the three escaped birds, though occasionally he would wake at night when he thought he heard a new phrase, a new word echo down the hallway toward his bedroom.

MEXICAN WRESTLERS

Twelve plastic wrestlers pinned to a strip of balsa wood, the hottest item in the tiendita, the wrestlers four inches tall—green, blue, and red masks hiding their rage, their muscled arms outstretched like Spider Man, spread legs taut against multi-colored tights. The wrestlers grab you as you walk into the store, make you buy them, so the set is always in demand. No one knows who each of the plastic figures is supposed to be. People buy them and dream of the mat, heavy arms and butts dropping with a slam as the crowd cheers and goes crazy. They guess at the names of the wrestlers—El Gato, El Chiva, Los Diablos, even Don Loco, El Perro, and Mister Tio Sam. I don't recall the others from my childhood days of watching Mexican wrestling on television. Perhaps now retired, Jose "El Burro" is not included in this set. The Medics were tag team champs in El Paso for years. One of them hid a steel plate in his shoe, opened opponents' heads when they fell, their manager finishing the victims with an umbrella through the ropes. We imitated The Medics, wore white shirts and masks to school for days, until we got thrown out of the ring, too, for violating the dress code. Wrestlers sweat over the booing crowd, one of them loving to flick the drops of sweat at people with his fingers, screaming when the seats clear. When my cousin Tony pinned me, I hated him for years. When my cousin choked and pinned me, I had no choice. I yanked his Halloween mask off. When I went back to the tiendita to get my own set of toy wrestlers, the last set had one figure missing, so I gently placed the group back on the shelf, turned around and went home.

JELLYFISH

The last jellyfish in the world was served to me in a strange restaurant in San Francisco. It glowed a deep blue and purple, and breathed on my plate. When I looked out the window, not knowing how to eat this thing, a man stood on the street corner looking in. We stared at each other, and I realized that he loved jellyfish. I waved him in and he did not hesitate to enter and sit at my table. I called the waiter for a second plate and sliced the quivering mess with my knife and fork. The man, a few years older than me, stared down at the jellyfish and wiped his lips. I slipped some pieces onto his plate and waited. His sleek, black hair curled over his eyebrows as he bent down and began to eat. I watched him slurp the jellyfish into his mouth, finishing his portion in seconds, not pausing as he reached for mine. I let him take my dish and wondered why I had ordered it off the menu in the first place. He dropped his fork loudly on his plate, stood up without a word, and walked out of the place. I sat there for several minutes and the man disappeared around the corner. I waited until the waiter brought the bill, got up, paid, and stepped outside. I found him lying dead on the street between two parked cars, several women screaming, the distant sound of a siren growing louder in the traffic. I stood by quietly as the police and ambulance came. No one questioned me in the small crowd. We all waited as they took him away on a stretcher. It's an incident I think about every now and then, the meal that could have been mine if I had not been so generous in my better days.

The home run ball rose over right field and disappeared before it started its downward arc. The right fielder backed to the warning path, but there was no ball to catch. He stood dazed as the roar of the crowd turned to confusion. Thousands of fans were on their feet for the home run. But, where was it? The hitter, a national hero who led the league in home runs, slowed to a hesitant jog as he rounded first base. The first and second basemen stood at their positions, one of them removing his cap from his head as he searched the night sky for the ball. The hitter nodded to the closest umpire, as if asking permission to keep running the bases, though he kept going. Managers, coaches, and players from both benches came out of the dugout. Unable to lower their heads from searching for the ball, some of the players stumbled over each other in front of the dugouts. The manager of the team at bat waved to his batter to keep running. The opposing manager ran toward one of the umpires. There was no ball, just the memory of the loud whack as the player's bat met the ball and sent it rocketing toward the right field bleachers. The ball's rapid trajectory was the last thing anyone recalled before it vanished. Thousands of witnesses amplified their stunned silence with a magnetic restlessness. With two men on base, the home run would give the visiting team a 3-2 lead in the first game of the World Series. It was the bottom half of the sixth inning. Where was the ball? As the hitter, his mouth agape, rounded third and headed home, the right fielder ran as fast as he could toward the second base umpire. With his confused manager joining him, both men screamed at the umpire to do something. The right fielder claimed the ball had not been hit hard enough for a home run. He screamed that he was in position to catch it when it vanished. His manager yelled that the three runs should not count because there was no ball hit out of the park. The opposing manager was welcoming his hero at home plate. He was not going to argue with anybody, even though he had no idea what had happened to the ball. In his book, it was a home run and the ball's speed and height made that obvious to the entire stadium before it disappeared. The beleaguered umpire at second base walked toward the umpire at first. He was surrounded by angry players and one red-faced manager. The first base umpire was coming to his defense when, suddenly, the ball appeared in the night sky. It fell where the right fielder was previously standing and settled in the warning path. Thousands of spectators saw it and both teams saw it. They pointed, screamed, and waved, but it was too late. The bases had been run, the three men had scored, and it would be ruled an inside-the-park home run. The last thing reported in the sports pages of every major newspaper was the right fielder running from the umpire he had been attacking, to the ball in the right field corner. He picked it out of the dirt and stared at it. What was not reported was his surprise at how old and yellow the baseball was. The stitches were coming off, and the ball was slightly warped. Some balls looked like that after a good hit, but this one was different. He threw it to the cut-off man at second, who also noticed how old the ball was. He picked it out of his glove and handed it to the umpire who was recovering from being attacked. When the umpire realized he had not seen this brand of baseball since his dirt lot days in the fifties, he tucked it into his coat pocket. The home plate umpire threw out another ball. When the papers carried the story, the second base umpire was surprised no sports writer asked him about the ball. Maybe it was because the home team won by a score of 5-3, three more runs coming on base hits. After the game, the umpire took his coat off in the umpire's dressing room and searched the pockets, but couldn't find the antique ball.

He ran down the muddy field and stayed ahead of the last defender. As the puddles from the driving rain splashed around the two of them, the pass came whistling through the watery air. He reached up as the ball emerged from the sheets of rain with no time on the clock. He felt the defender ride his back the moment before the ball stopped in his straining hands. They both went down in a roar from the crowd and what sounded like a pounding ocean. He hung onto the ball and slid into the end zone in a drowning wave of water. He couldn't stop his moving body or close his mouth as water poured down his throat. The defender slipped away, and he felt himself slowing down, the ball clutched tightly to his chest. He lay there coughing for a long time as teammates piled on and the loud thundering from the crowd exploded through his helmet. They lifted him in their arms and carried him off the field. He gasped for air and spit up water. The ball fell out of his grip, but a tangle of arms pushed it back into him. He wanted to stand and throw up the last of the water, but his buddies would not let him down. They held him in the air and paraded him around the sidelines bench. With one free arm, he managed to crawl off someone's shoulder pads and find the muddy ground. He slipped and sat in a quagmire of mud and football shoes. The legs moved in and stood him up. The game was over, and they had won the championship on the last play. All he could mutter and cough was the word "yes" several times, but the blistering sound of the hometown crowd muted his participation. Through watery eyes, he saw his coach come up and hug him in a tight, painful embrace. He kept his helmet on and the ball close to his chest as his teammates knelt in the traditional post game prayer. No one cared that they were kneeling in a moat of water and mud. They bowed their heads and the rain continued to fall as the team offered prayer in thanks for the victory. As the coach finished the prayer, the whole team whooped, screamed, and flew out of the water in one motion. It was over. He jogged off the field with his teammates, the explosions of lights, banners, and waving students making him dizzy. It felt like the dressing room doors were miles away as he slowed to a walk and held the football high in the air. The crowd went wilder as he waved the ball over his head. He was surrounded by players, and only ten yards from the concrete tunnel that led to the dressing rooms, when he fell dead in the mud. For one instant, no one noticed or looked down. Several celebrating players jumped over him laughing at him to get up. It took another minute before people started screaming at the motionless body lying face down in the foaming grass. When teammates and coaches ran to him, dozens of fans were already leaping off the bleachers to encircle the scene. It was reported later that the bullet entered the right side of his helmet and killed him instantly. The shot came from a high powered rifle up in the stands. Trajectory tests might pinpoint the approximate rows in the bleachers, but police were not sure of finding the killer among the thousands who attended the game. Months of interviews with hundreds of fans who were on that side of the stadium went nowhere. One year later, they renamed the stadium after him. Two years later, the city championship trophy was renamed in his honor. His school fired the football coach after a 4-6 and 2-8 win-loss record in the two seasons following his death.

BASKETBALL

The two men are playing a sweaty, hard one-on-one game. Their t-shirts are drenched and their bald heads glisten in the gym lights. One man is black, the other white, but the score is tied seven to seven. There is no one else in the gym, except a seven year old black kid who sits high in the empty rafters, his eyes glued to the magnificent sight on the slick floor. The black man takes the rebound from the other guy's missed shot and comes back to the boundary line. He twists and grunts, then pulls a fast one to the left of his opponent. The white guy does his knee thing and sends the other one flying on his ass. They laugh at each other, obviously having fun, familiar with each other's game. The standing player extends a hand to his partner who is on his ass under the basket. He helps him up, not expecting the knee in the groin. When the white guy goes down, the little boy stands up, a look of recognition on his face. The black guy holds the basketball in his large hands and grins at the wriggling body on the floor. The white guy rolls onto his side, his knees bunched into his stomach, and he lets out a groan that echoes across the empty building. The kid slowly walks down the bleachers, sits on the bottom row and tightens the laces on his sneakers. The black man notices him for the first time and stops smiling. He waves him onto the court. The kid jogs out to meet him as the suffering white guy rolls out of the picture and staggers off to the showers. The triumphant black guy throws the basketball hard at his new opponent and is surprised to see the kid pluck it before it hits him in the chest. The seven year old comes on in a whirlwind of basketball moves. In a few minutes, the score is five to one in favor of the kid. He has blocked, stolen, and out-rebounded the man, who is dragging himself around the boundary line, his breath coming long and hard.

When it is nine to two, the black man leans over as if to hurl his lunch and signals he has had enough. He holds out a hand to the kid who approaches him. Thinking they are going to shake on it, the black man has his guard down. In an instant, the kid throws the basketball in the guy's face and runs off. The black man falls back with a cry as six guys in game jerseys appear from the shadows of the bleachers. They rush the court with enthusiasm and grab the ball from the staggering figure. They are his age, a mix of black and white dudes who break into a three on three game without paying further attention to the beaten man. As he moves off the court, he glances up at the dark bleachers and gasps in shock to find over two hundred people sitting in the stands, not one of them making a sound, their faces frozen, their hands folded calmly on their laps, row upon stuffed row of black and white faces following him as he exits toward the quiet showers.

BOWLING ALLEY

Without knowing why, I stop at a bowling alley in a part of town I have never been in, park my car and go inside. I am startled to find my father's trophies lining every glass case in the joint. There are tournament championships for individual and team play. Every single trophy has my father's name imprinted on it. The dozens of men and women bowling in the crowded place don't know anything about this. I want to ask one of the attendants how they got my father's trophies, but none of them are around. The lanes are filled with bowlers, there are people waiting for an open slot, and there are shelves of many-colored balls lining the entire lobby. I spot a young guy with a company logo on his t-shirt and go down to the lane where he is talking to a group of bowlers. Before I can tap him on the shoulder, I am surrounded by two beefy guys who tell me their team is one player short and they want me to fill in. They don't listen when I tell them I haven't bowled in fifteen years. Team t-shirts and shoes are thrown into my arms, the guys slap me on the back, and order me a beer. They even find me a heavy, old black bowling ball and drop it in the ditch of balls that surrounds the scoring machine and screen projector. I get dressed and sit on the warm bench, waiting my turn. The constant explosions of pins and the thud of bowling balls as they are launched down the alleys keep me company. When the guys motion that it is my turn, I find my ball, shake a little, and do my best to present a true bowler's form. I do the quick steps, arch my right hand back, and release as hard as I can. The ball shoots down the center of the alley and the sound of my first strike shatters the air, my team cheering wildly as I step off the platform. This goes on all night. In my first game, I hit four strikes in a row, miss a few, and wind up with eight strikes. I am the hero. By the time the night is over, I have led my drunk team to victory, am sauced myself, and haven't even told anyone my name. I stumble up the carpeted stairs, grab my street shoes, and manage to put them on. As I head out the door into the cool night, I pass the large display case by the front doors and find my father's trophies are gone. The replacements have names I do not know. My father's name is no longer embossed on the gold plates of each trophy. I go out into the night and fall into my vehicle in time to hear my car phone ring. It is my mother and she is crying as she says, "Your father is in the hospital. He is dying. You'd better come quick."

FIREFLIES

I am running around the jogging track at a park
in my neighborhood, the summer evening drawing two other run-
ners, a woman running alone on the other side of the oval, and an
older man a few yards behind her. The grass in the middle of the
track and the surrounding park is glittering with fireflies—little
flashes of humidity in the oncoming darkness, lighting my effort to
get around the track twice. I huff and puff, and three streaks of light
cross my path, then go out. I think I hear a shout and look to my left
where the woman, in halter top and tiny gym shorts, has picked up
the pace, the man about twenty yards behind her slowing almost to
a walk, his belly bouncing with each step, his long, hairy legs pale
sticks against the growing number of fireflies. I start my slow jog
around the curve and get a better view of the woman, who is way
across the track, a figure as tiny as the fireflies that criss-cross the
grass, weaving in the distance like the bright future of my struggle to
lose weight. The old man, fifty yards ahead of me, stumbles on the
red gravel that fills the lanes. One Reebok goes flying as he rolls for
a couple of yards, pulls himself up and grabs his shoe without missing
a beat. I don't know if I should stop and see if he is okay, because he
keeps running, this momentary obstacle giving him new energy as he
sprints away from my approaching misery. As early evening deepens
into the purple hue before nightfall, dozens of fireflies lace the
length of the track, and the old man vanishes among their streaks.
The blonde is coming around behind me, her figure weaving in and
out of firefly fire, the increase in the flashes of light startling me, as
if a snowstorm of silver was falling on the entire park. I keep jogging,
trying to go faster, but my heart is pounding and my sweatband is not
keeping the sweat out of my stinging eyes. I enter and exit firefly

space, several of the insects hovering around my head, one of them so close I can see the electric charge bristling through its tiny being, my legs hurting as I try to close the gap between myself and the old man, while keeping the young woman behind me. I see the next curve growing toward me as two fireflies crash into the red gravel. The blonde is going to lap me, and I look for the old man on the other side of the track. I can't see him through the thickening threads of fireflies. Perhaps he quit and walked away, his humiliation complete. Maybe he ran to the water fountain by the bathrooms on the other side of the swing sets. I can't find him as approaching footsteps crunch gravel rapidly and I smell the sweat of the woman behind me—a fine and arrogant mix of female energy and Nordstrom's perfume. I am slowing down in the rain of fireflies, the blonde yards behind me, but I do not move over. She closes the distance, heaving and grunting. She shoves me aside with two open palms. I stumble like the old man, but don't fall, instead bouncing back to grab the woman as she goes by. All I can manage is a short pull on her halter, but it is enough. She twists away slapping at me and her top comes off. She springs away like a rubber band, the two of us moving our feet the whole time, the release out of her wet, black thing sending me flying into the grass. I roll and break, my face sliding into the sweet dampness of green, this crash landing awakening the thousands of fireflies hiding in the lawn. I slide to a stop on the green, my skin burning, the air a pulsing stream of flashing momentum, the entire park igniting in fireflies, the topless blonde way down on the other side, too far for me to see her in detail as she finds the old man who has been resting by the trees. I can barely see through the soothing stream of fireflies all around me, endless hits of light bouncing off my broken body as the sweating woman puts an arm around the old man and leads him away.

BIG CHIEF TABLETS

I find a Big Chief writing tablet in my room like the ones I used to have when I was a kid. I have not seen these tablets in over thirty years and this one on my desk smells fresh and new. I have no idea who put it there, because I didn't buy it. I take one of my favorite pens and start to doodle on the first page of the tan-colored sheet with the big blue lines. The circles, triangles, and odd faces I draw are the kind I always doodle before starting to write. I flip through a few pages in the tablet because I like the sound of the flapping sheets. I want to write a poem, but only a few words come out—inside, tree, future, horn. I stop and go back to the first page of doodles, but they have changed. There is now a perfect ink drawing of the Mona Lisa on the sheet. It has been drawn in the same green ink as the pen I hold in my hand. I stare at this famous masterpiece. My own doodles surround the smiling face. I grab the tablet as it starts to slip from my lap, accidentally ripping the page. The tear moves through some of my own doodles, but does not touch the Mona Lisa. I close the tablet and turn on my computer. I wait the few seconds to call up my word processing program and pop in a disc of new writing I have been working on. Instead of the familiar clouds of the Microsoft logo, the Mona Lisa appears on the screen. This time, she is holding the Big Chief tablet in her hands. The famous red cover with the Indian face is held close to her heart. I stare at the screen, hit a button, and a boxed message comes on: Disk Error. Unable to recover. The disc contains some of the best poems I have written in months and I have not created a back-up disc. I try to get out of the program, but it is frozen, and I have no choice but to pull out the disc and reboot. This I do with no problem, then go back into the restarted computer. I call up a file with my favorite new poem on it and see it is an early version that was not damaged. I have no copy of the revisions, so I print the poem in hope of recalling how I revised it. The sheet comes out as a colored print of the Big Chief. The smiling Indian holds a framed picture of the Mona Lisa in his dark hands and the revision I thought I had lost is held up in the Mona Lisa's hands.

THE BINOCULARS

Through the binoculars, he saw a diamond shaped toad flying above the pond. He adjusted the focus and watched the toad hit the water and break into slivers of purple and yellow, the threads melting as they rippled beyond his sight. He lowered the binoculars and tried to get closer, but the swamp was too deep. Then he heard the noise for the second time that day and peered through the binoculars again. The willow tree shimmered with trails of ladybugs that clung to the swinging branches of the tree. He extended the telescopic sight and the lens drew closer to the climbing ladybugs so that the strange markings on their red shells became visible. He centered on one ladybug and read the word "condition" on its back. He lowered the binoculars and the willow tree stood perfectly still, again too far on the other side of the water for him to go collect a ladybug as proof. He heard the noise for the third time, but could not find its source. He threw his head back to the sky and gazed through the binoculars at a blue heron. It was a huge prehistoric looking bird whose massive wings flapped as if time stood still. He followed it through the sharp glass and there was a pair of headphones in the heron's beak. They resembled the kind you would wear listening to a Walkman or portable CD player. As the heron flew into the distance, it let go of the headphones. He followed the plastic cord through the binoculars until it hit the water, and the splash ignited the wilderness in a blaring rock and roll song, electric guitar feedback and screeching singers making him drop the binoculars and run.

BLACK ANGEL WITH
WHITE GUITAR

When the rooms shook, I was afraid. I believed too deeply, saw my escape entangled in the strange wires that led to white contradictions cutting into the chests of black and brown men. When my ears bled, I was brave and gave the wah-wah pedal time to heal me, taking me back to the first time I ever heard one. When it exploded, I harmed myself by devouring the amps and plugging in more guitars. The cry was loud, black and electrocuted—axis, bold as love. It had to do with the wires, how they snapped with vibrations that killed the instinct to flee. The cry had to do with love, wide-open mouth that emerges when the frets lose control. When the rooms shook, I was afraid and could not acknowledge the lyrics nor turn up the volume, could only stare at the black shape igniting his guitar on stage. It gave me my teen-age body wrapped in bright red, lavender and yellow scarves. It fell back, never saw the advantage of hiding behind the amps or burning in the spotlight. When I saw it was not a shape, but a body, I was too late. This happened in the days of wings. It was too late. This was in the days of wings when the shattering roar of boiling guitars was the sacrifice that betrayed me. I stood farther back from the stage. I had no hair. My eyes were red and knew the lyrics. For one moment, they saw the white guitar.

circling the tortilla dragon

PART FOUR

THE JUKEBOX

Fernando drops a dime in the old jukebox and finds a Johnny Cash song he likes. The saloon is quiet in the early afternoon, only three guys hunched over their beers at the bar. Fernando flips the metal holders that list the songs and keeps looking for the obscure Neil Young tune, "Sugar Mountain," which he found in a whorehouse bar in Juarez long ago. He searches for the song in every jukebox he finds in these places. He has never found "Sugar Mountain" again, though "I Walk the Line" by Cash is a favorite in every joint. Fernando sits at his stool as Johnny's booming voice cuts through the drowsy place. He has always wondered why a whorehouse jukebox would stock a hard-to-find Neil Young song. It has been thirty years since he came across it. Fernando drinks his beer and thinks about those high school days when he and Guillermo would go to Juarez every weekend to get drunk and laid. They were crazy times, but every guy at school knew about Juarez. He takes another sip and mouths the words in the Cash song, as he recalls the night he and Guillermo got lost trying to get back to El Paso. They couldn't find the main street to the international bridge. As they stumbled through the warm July night, the sound of laughter and conjunto music led them to a tiny cantina they had never visited. Inside was the biggest, shiniest jukebox Fernando had ever seen. It was the size of a refrigerator, with blinking lights and row upon row of hit songs. Fernando leaned into the glass as Guillermo went to order beers. He was amazed at the selection of songs. Thirty years later, he could not recall any of them. All he remembers is dropping the coins in, the sudden start of a fast song, and the woman in the blue light of the back room—the vibrating jukebox, the music tearing the walls apart, exposing him as he lay on top of the woman. The blue lights turned green, then red, and back to blue as shouting men crashed through the broken walls. What happened next is a blur in Fernando's memory, the fast action of being beaten in the alley by two Federales now a blur as Johnny Cash's song ends and the bar is quiet. Fernando goes to the jukebox and tosses in another coin. He flips through the charts. About to give up, he comes to the last sheet of songs. There it is. Neil Young's "Sugar Mountain." How could he have missed it? He punches the two white buttons and waits. He can hear Neil's acoustic guitar and first low words, "Oh, to live on Sugar Mountain with the barkers and the colored balloons. You can be twenty on Sugar Mountain, though you think you're leaving there too soon." But, the song does not start. He only hears it in his head. He waits. The song does not play. He turns to the bartender, but he has gone into the back room. Fernando kicks the jukebox. No "Sugar Mountain." The lights on the machine are blinking and the men at the bar are waiting. A different song comes on—"Secret Agent Man" by Johnny Rivers. He hates that song! Where is "Sugar Mountain?" Fernando turns and faces the large room and is surprised at how quickly every stool at the bar has filled with quiet, drinking men.

CIRCLING THE
TORTILLA DRAGON

Lencho circles the tortilla dragon, approaches it warily as its steam and power rises above the stove in the hot kitchen. Lencho has slain many tortilla dragons before and this one is as powerful as the ones in his past. He circles the tortilla dragon and keeps himself from making a mistake. He must not allow his watering mouth to touch the delicate flesh of the freshly made tortillas today. He has to circle and circle because the tortilla dragon is growing larger and larger in the kitchen. It resembles the dark brown and black patches Lencho has interpreted on his grandmother's tortillas since he was a boy. This dragon is a combination of those brown and black shapes he always loved to lick with his tongue, the burnt taste telling him it was a good tortilla. As he gets hungrier, Lencho circles the tortilla dragon, knowing the flames of this powerful force can cook him faster than a tortilla. He turns and turns in the kitchen, recalls how a tortilla dragon will strike when you least expect it. Lencho pauses and this is his first mistake. The source of his yearning lunges forward and takes him. He struggles to get away from the sharp claws and awful gas of the enormous dragon's mouth. Before he realizes what has caught him, Lencho finds himself bent over the ancient kitchen stove, his face only three inches from the hot plate where his grandmother bakes her tortillas. The burner is on high and the black iron reverberates with a magnetic force that pulls Lencho within inches of his tortilla life. He tries to fight the pull toward the heat, but the dragon has him by the throat. Lencho can feel its scaly body pressing on his back, trying to flatten his face on the hot plate like a tortilla he will never eat. Then, suddenly, the tortilla dragon lets go of its grip and Lencho is thrown across the kitchen. He tumbles backward over a chair and lands in a heap against a corner. Dazed, he looks up in time to see heavy smoke rising from the stove. A tortilla is burning. He struggles to his feet and makes it to the stove. In his rush to save the burning tortilla, which wasn't there when the dragon tried to fry his face, Lencho momentarily forgets the creature is still in the room. As he pulls the scorched thing from the hot plate, the thick smell of burnt flour overcomes him. He turns in time to meet the massive tortilla dragon. Lencho shoves the burned tortilla into the creature's open mouth and it chokes on the black chips and ashes. It rears back, knocks the kitchen table aside, and the room fills with smoke. Lencho can hardly see, but he thinks the dragon has crawled out the front door. He grabs two fresh tortillas off the stack his grandmother made a half hour earlier and runs outside. He is too late. The dragon has disappeared. Lencho eats the two tortillas as the burnt air behind him reshapes itself, the first long curves of heavy wings starting to appear in the blue smoke of the quiet kitchen.

MISTAKES

Henry made the mistake of walking in on David and Lencha, Henry's girlfriend. They were doing it on the floor, and Henry made the mistake of forgetting there was a full moon that night. He made the wrong choice of grabbing the naked David and tossing him through the open window. The guy landed in the rose bushes and never came back. Henry made the error of forgiving Lencha, who didn't know about him and Sophie, but he never did trust her again. Henry was in error when he quit his job as a car mechanic and went to work for Heavy Sanchez, his old buddy from high school. Before Henry knew it, he had taken the wrong path and was making too much money pushing coke. His new car and clothes caught the attention of the guys in the suits, who followed him all the time. Henry spoke words he shouldn't have on his cell phone and let the suits know where he was meeting Lencha's father, who did not choose wisely by liking his daughter's boyfriend too much. That night, Henry made a wrong turn on the way to the rendezvous near Copia and Alameda streets and was late. The suits thought everyone was there and busted several guys, including Lencha's father, but Henry was busy making a U-turn near the railroad tracks and missed the bust by three minutes. He drove the wrong way, turning into a dark alley when he spotted the police cars, but it was a dead end and he had to stop between narrow brick walls covered in graffiti. He got out of the car and took a peek around the corner at the police action. It was one block down and he couldn't tell who got busted. As he huddled in the shadows, he was dressed in the wrong clothes because four dudes appeared out of nowhere and jumped him. Henry decided to fight back with his kick boxing lessons and took two of them down before making the untaught move of slipping and falling. As he went down, the gun in his pants went off and killed the third homeboy as the fourth ran. Henry hurried to his car and jumped in, but the gunshot drew the attention of the suits who were almost done with their bust. They made the tactical error of getting to the alley too late because Henry was gone, his panic giving him the skill to drive his car out of the alley in reverse. Henry lay low for awhile, but selected to think with his dick instead of his brain and went to bed with Marina, David's ex. The hidden video camera caught everything, but the guy who set it up for David read the instructions incorrectly and placed the camera lens at an angle that caught close ups of the lovers' asses, not their faces. Henry never found out about it because he never saw Marina again, deciding to leave town instead. He ran around Los Angeles for a few weeks, trying to connect with cool people. When he found the right circle of friends and started delivering stuff again, he was the last minute substitute driver for a key delivery to a very rich and powerful client who made the mistake of paying thousands in cash before seeing the goods. Henry worked at night for his new boss, but this client only did business during the day and the regular day driver was out sick. Being new to southern California, Henry got lost on the way to the rendezvous with the client, and took the Santa Ana freeway, a route he rarely took. Part of the freeway collapsed and it took two days to find the remains of Henry's car under the concrete, his body smashed so flat, it was hard to pick the bones from the forty pounds of cocaine spread all over the wreckage like a white cloud sending Henry to heaven. By the way, his boss made the mistake of creating the impression he thought it was cool to rip people off and was shot dead in his elegant home on the day after one of the largest earthquakes in modern history hit L.A.

THE TESTAMENT
OF SANTO

The testament of Santo was found four years ago in a paperbag by the side of Highway 114 near Aguirre Springs, New Mexico. The yellow sheet in Santo's handwriting reads: "I swear to my God I saw the lights on the mountain that night and they went up the cliffs. When I followed them in my car, I had a flat tire and pulled over to the side of the road. I was changing the flat with my headlights on when I heard someone laughing in the canyons. It was a terrible laugh and scared me. I put the spare on and got in the car, but it wouldn't start. I kept turning the engine, until this flash of blue light exploded across the steering wheel and the image of La Virgen de Guadalupe appeared on my windshield. I made the sign of the cross and jumped out of the car. The headlights turned off by themselves and I tripped over some cactus because it was so dark. I lay there out of breath and heard footsteps near me. I couldn't see anything except the incredible stars in the sky. Then, I felt the cold hand on my neck. I cried out and the hand let go. I ran to my car, raised the windows and locked the doors. Was this happening just because I had wanted to see those lights? I looked at the image of La Virgin, which was starting to fade on the windshield, and I calmed down. I tried the engine one more time and it started! I got out of there as quickly as I could, but had gone only a couple of miles down the highway when I felt there was someone in the car with me. I looked in the rearview mirror and the face of an ugly, shriveled woman stared at me. I screamed, and the old woman, covered in muddy rags, opened her door and flew into the night. I hit the gas and was lucky there was hardly any traffic on the road because my car was weaving from lane to lane. I could see the lights of Las Cruces in the distance and they made me feel better. I noticed my fuel gauge was almost empty. There was no way I wanted to run out of gas out here, so I pulled into the first service station I came to. It was an old Shell station with two pumps next to an old, white building. The lights were on and there was somebody inside, so I got out and began to fill up. As I pumped the gas, I looked toward the Organ Mountains. The dancing lights were still there like blue dots running up and down the mountains. I filled the tank and went inside to pay. There was no one behind the counter, so I waited and heard a noise in the back room. Two guys in Shell uniforms came out and pointed guns at me and asked for my money. I told them I had enough for gas and a Coke. They laughed and shot me. I fell down and held hands with the shriveled woman as she led me across the shallow arroyo leading to the blue lights on the mountain. Before we reached the top, I wrote these words down and put them in my sack. I threw it down the rocky slope and watched it roll toward the highway, turned to the dancing lights on the high cliffs and saw myself standing at the top.

THE RED HORSE

Manolo saw a man on a red horse riding on the bluff above the road where he walked. He wondered who the horseman was because the sunlight on the stranger's head bristled with blinding stars and kept him from identifying the rider who headed down to the road to block Manolo's path. Manolo's eyes watered as the horse reared back and neighed, the burning rider spreading smoke on the road. The curtain of darkness kept Manolo from moving on, not knowing the red horse and rider saved him from the earthquake ahead, his entire family crushed in the ruins, the town destroyed, Manolo falling on the ground and shaking in a cloud of smoke that took hours to lift. Years later, Manolo still sees the horse every now and then, when he walks along the river of his new country. It has no rider of fire as it grazes alone on the other side of the water, his second wife and children waiting for the right time to ask the quiet Manolo about the red tattoo of the animal branded on his chest.

MAN GOING TO BED

A man gets ready to go to sleep and pulls back the covers to find a large, black scorpion in the middle of his bed. It is six inches long, one of the biggest he has seen in this part of the country, its charcoal color very unusual. Most of the scorpions in the region are a pale fleshy tone. The tail of the ugly thing rises in the air to show the man what it has to offer. He stands by his bed and contemplates the scorpion, figures his family is up to something again. The man goes to the bathroom cabinet, finds a jar he keeps there for these kinds of things and returns to his bedroom. The scorpion is gone. He did not expect this, because, in the past, they have always waited for him. He carefully moves the blanket off the bed and shakes it. Nothing. He removes the clean sheets, but can't find the scorpion. He gets down on his knees and peeks under the bed. It is early enough in the evening to see under it, but he makes sure by grabbing a flashlight from the nightstand. He sweeps the beam under the bed, but no scorpion. He can't search any longer because he has to get up early tomorrow and go to work. He takes his clothes off, carefully hangs everything in the closet, and puts his shoes on top of the dresser. He knows by now not to leave anything on the floor. He gets into bed, pulls up the sheets and blanket, and turns off the light. In the growing darkness of early evening, it is too hot for so many blankets and sheets. After all, it is summertime and that is why there are scorpions in the house. He has trouble falling asleep, but finally dozes off. During the night, he tosses and turns, but will not remember these turnings when he wakes the next day. Around two or three in the morning, the man is lying on his back snoring when the scorpion returns. It crawls across the foot of the bed and moves up the man's legs. The man is under a thin, cool sheet when this happens. The scorpion inspects the breathing body as it crosses the man's belly and stops to rest on his chest. The man's face jerks for a second, the scorpion's tail comes up in warning, but nothing happens as the man continues to sleep. His arms are casually stretched on either side of his body. The scorpion starts again, moves onto the left side of the man's face, crosses his shoulder and settles on the pillow. The scorpion doesn't even raise its tail when the man turns to his right, away from the creature, and keeps sleeping. The scorpion continues its night journey by leaving the man's bed and climbing up the wall. By early morning, it is on the ceiling beyond the bed. When the man wakes up, he spots the scorpion right away and does not hurry. He keeps an eye on it while he puts his clothes on. It must be sleeping, the man thinks. He finds the large jar from the bathroom and takes the broom he keeps in the hallway. Holding the open jar in his left hand, he nudges the scorpion with the broom in his right. It points its tail downward and springs, misses the jar by a few inches, and lands with a thud on the carpeted floor. In his impatience, the man swats it with the broom. It takes three fast strikes to kill it. By the time he is done, the man has deconstructed the thing into several awful pieces. He picks up the enormous stiff tail with the end of the broom and goes into the kitchen, where he drops it into a second waiting jar full of old, wrinkled scorpion tails. He dresses for work, leaves the house on time, and is not there when an unidentified member of his estranged family breaks into the house and releases another scorpion. As the mysterious member of the man's family leaves, this second huge scorpion can't be seen as it slowly turns the same red color as the blanket on the bed.

BELLYBUTTON

Julia told her grandson Alfredo his belly button was a gift, but did not say where the gift came from. One night, she put him to bed and Alfredo raised his t-shirt to stare at his belly button. "Why is it a gift, Grandma?" he asked. "Who gave it to me?' The old woman smiled at Alfredo. "The earth gave you your ombligo." Alfredo did not understand. "The earth?" His grandmother tucked him in and ran her hand over his forehead. "When your mother had you, I took a handful of mud from our garden and rubbed it on her belly." "You did?" Alfredo's eyes widened. "Yuck! Didn't that make her dirty?" His grandmother laughed. "No, Alfredo. Your mother needed her mother to help her bring you to us." She sat on the edge of the bed, made sure her grandson was covered by the blanket and told him about the mud that helped his birth. She said when the rains came, families were ready to bring their sons and daughters into the world. The mothers could not give birth until their mothers covered them with soft mud from the gardens surrounding their houses. It was the only way to assure a safe birth, even if the mud washed off before delivery. Mothers and daughters had been doing this for generations. Alfredo's mother, Lencha, followed her mother into their garden hours before Alfredo's birth. Julia and her daughter knew it was time by the way the sun baked the mud left by the rainstorm that morning. The women removed their shoes and stepped into a puddle. They held hands and splashed their feet. Mud flew up and covered them. Julia stepped out of the puddle, reached down with both hands and grabbed the dripping mud. Lencha leaned back to let her mother rub her stomach with the dark, sticky earth. "The earth is clean, Lencha," Julia said. Lencha stood there with her round belly, then bowed down to grab more mud. Both women were silent as the daughter applied mud to her mother. Julia's thin stomach was completely covered with a shiny layer. "The earth is clean, Mama," Lencha whispered. Julia had nodded and embraced her daughter. Now she described this moment to Alfredo, who listened quietly. "But why is the earth clean when there is so much dirt?" he asked. Julia laughed. "Yes, Alfredo, there is a lot of dirt, but it is on the ground to show us how many boys have been born." Alfredo yawned and thought about these things. "But how did I get my belly-button? Did it come from the dirt?" Julia shook her head. "No, Alfredo. Your ombligo is a sign the earth let go of you as a gift to your mother." Julia continued, "When the mud covered your mother's stomach, it released its spirit into her body. When a baby is born, the ombligo is the arm of the earth letting go. The hands I used to cover your mother with mud and the hands of the earth held each other through your belly button." Alfredo's eyes lit up. "Like shaking hands!" he exclaimed. Julia smiled and loved the boy more. "Yes, like shaking hands. Your ombligo is the spot where your mother shook hands with the earth. When you are born, the handshake is over and your belly button is left as a sign your mother and the earth agreed to bring you to us." Alfredo studied his ombligo, then pulled the blanket up to his chin. "Goodnight, Grandma," he said. "Goodnight, Alfredo," Julia whispered. She leaned over him and kissed him on the forehead. As she started to leave, Alfredo asked, "Grandma?" She paused in the doorway. "Did your mother shake hands with the earth when you were born, too?" Julia nodded. "Yes, she did that a long time ago." "So, the earth is older than you?" Alfredo asked in wonder. His grandmother laughed. "Yes, the earth is older than your grandmother. Goodnight, Alfredo." The boy sighed deeply as she closed the door.

THE BABY

The baby wore a moustache and beard in the dream. It had a man's face. It looked up at me and said in a deep voice, "You're such a baby, you look like your father." The baby startled me by knowing who I was. I could not tell if someone was holding the baby in his or her arms. There was a cloud or mist surrounding the child as it lay or floated in smooth blue blankets. It looked at me with a very serious expression. It was a man's expression, not a baby's. I had no idea who he was. Could he have inherited the looks of men of my family? Was this my father as a child? To him, I was the child because he said I was the "baby," though he recognized that I resembled my father. But, how did he know I had those features? Where had he come from before he appeared to me? Why the moustache and hair on his face? The deep voice? The statement of acknowledgment? How far back was I supposed to go, in order to agree with the baby? How far back did the maturity on his face take me before I could nod silently, in the dream, and wait for the baby to speak again?

I am one of the Indians about to be discovered by Christopher Columbus. I stand on the beach with my fellow tribesmen as three giant white birds come across the sea toward us. Some warriors become frightened and run when they see what is approaching. Some of us stand proudly, ready to fight these creatures with our spears and arrows. As they come closer, we realize they are not birds, but larger versions of our own boats. We mumble and whisper, a serious dread settling into our hearts. We wait. Somebody signals that there is a small boat approaching. Soon, we gaze at the first white men we have ever seen. There are eight of them in the boat and they have long sticks. They wave to us in a peaceful manner. There are over one hundred of us waiting as the eight strange men splash ashore. One of them acts like their leader because none of the men step in front of him. They are covered in sheets of shiny rock. Even their faces are partly hidden inside the rocks they wear on their heads. Our chief steps forward with three of his closest warriors who point their spears at the white leader. The two chiefs face each other. Our confused cries die down and complete silence overtakes this encounter. All I can hear are the soothing rhythms of the waves as they hit the shore. Suddenly, both sides are shocked out of their defiant silence when an enormous, loud bird appears in the sky. I look up and see a bird of glistening rock, similar to what these white men are wearing, as it zooms over our heads and across the beach. It has two sets of long, straight wings, one above the other. There is a man sitting on the head of this bird. He looks down and waves at us, his face hidden behind a yellow mask. The bird is on fire and trailing a string of black smoke as it heads toward the water. Both worlds watch as it crashes into the sea and explodes in a huge fireball. We've

circling the tortilla dragon

had enough. The white men follow their frantic leader back to their boat. My chief is nowhere to be found, so we run and hide in the trees. Someone points to the tiny man from the rock bird who is descending from the sky, a white cloud tied to his body. A fury of arrows greets him from the trees, while fire sticks and whistling stones erupt from the strangers' boat, but nothing stops this flying man from getting closer to the earth, to us. We stay in the trees as he hits the water near the escaping boat of rock men. His enormous white cloud slowly descends after him and covers the boat, the desperate cries of these creature men the last sound we hear as we run to protect our village.

SNOWSTORM

It is snowing as I reach the house. I knock and knock, heavy snow falling off my hooded parka, my legs cold and shaking despite the heavy coat. I keep knocking, until a woman opens the door, but she does not recognize me. I say her name several times, but she will not let me into her house, though this is where I was told in her phone call to appear. I plead and beg, having thrown my hood onto my shoulders so she can get a good look at my shivering face. Suddenly, she recognizes me and begins to unbutton her sweater. I am standing in the snow outside and this woman is taking off her clothes! I don't know what to do, so I push my way through the huge drift that has collected in the doorway. She stops undressing and goes into the kitchen, her jeans dragging on the floor, caught on one foot. I pull my parka off and shake the snow off my boots, a large puddle in the foyer forming around my feet. I hear sounds in the kitchen, but don't know what to do. Before I can decide, she returns completely naked. This woman has been my friend for many years and has never done this before. She says in a calm voice, "I have been taken prisoner by pirates." I blink at this beautiful woman and don't know what to say. Finally, I manage to ask, "What do you want me to do?" She gestures to the wall near the staircase, where a black pirate flag with skull and crossbones is pinned. "Take your clothes off and put that on," she commands. I blubber some noise from my mouth, but get undressed. She studies me with no emotion as I fumble out of my wet clothes. When I am ready, I pad over to the flag, unpin it from the wall and cover myself with it. It hangs to the floor and I shiver in my bare feet, careful to avoid the melting ice from my boots. Suddenly, she snaps her fingers and yells, "All right!" Fourteen of my best friends come bounding down the stairs in pirate outfits, men and women shouting, "Happy Birthday! Happy Birthday!" I stand naked in my flag, my face red, the naked woman now covered with a blanket by her husband, whose expression says he can't believe she did this, my friends dancing and popping champagne corks all over the room, two of them having disappeared down the hallway with my clothes.

DIEGO

Diego Rivera sits high atop the scaffold and watches his assistant work on the mural. His wide back and the seat of his pants expand over the thin boards of the scaffold. Diego's sleeves are rolled up and he holds a pallet of paint in his left arm, a paintbrush in his right. He has been working for two months on this mural in the San Francisco Institute of Art and things are starting to happen. Frida is spending more time alone, going off on excursions by herself, or hiding in her room claiming she is not feeling well. The other morning when he arrived at six A.M. to work on the mural before his two assistants got there, Diego saw something move high up on the wall. He retreated several yards back from the mural and looked up at the miners and highrise construction workers he had painted in the top left corner. He swears one of them moved like he was about to fall from the girders twenty floors above the earth. Diego climbed the scaffold carefully that morning, his heavy weight making it difficult to work on the narrow boards. He reached the second level and spotted a tiger coming out of one hard-hatted man. Diego glared at this freshly drawn detail. Where had this tiger come from? Neither Neto nor David, his assistants, would do such a thing to Diego's work. What was this tiger doing emerging from the head of the construction worker Diego had labored to get right? He spent most of the day erasing the tiger and redoing the male figure. Last night, Frida took her clothes off and told Diego she was going to parade down the San Francisco streets naked. Diego sat up in bed, tired from a long day at the mural, and gave a frustrated sigh. Frida spun around like a ballerina, teasing Diego to do something. Of course, nothing happened. Nothing had happened for a long time. The two slept peacefully after Frida quit dancing nude and came to bed. The two of them held each other and fell asleep. One week after finding the tiger, Diego arrives late in the morning. Neto is already there, waiting for him with great anxiety. David has the day off. When Diego walks into the small gym where the mural is being painted, Neto points to the bottom right corner of the mural. "What now?" Diego asks, and then sees the huge gray rat someone has painted crawling along one of the steel girders. He holds his head in both hands. Frida? A trick of Frida's? No, she may hate him, but she would never touch his work. Diego bends down and studies the realistic rat that has appeared in his grand vision of industrial America. For an instant, Diego likes it and wants to laugh. He tells Neto to white-wash it. Neto nods, but when he picks up a can of white paint, Diego changes his mind. "Leave it," he tells Neto, whose eyes bug out at this command. Diego chuckles and goes out into the courtyard of the art school building. Giant palm trees, mimosas, and bleeding heart plants line the four walls of the courtyard. Diego goes to the north wall and takes a black marker pen out of his shirt pocket. Below a classroom window, he moves aside some mimosa leaves that touch the building and draws a caricature of himself and Frida having sex. The black ink from the pen seeps quickly into the dry brick. In less than two minutes, he sketches the figures in their wildest coupling. He signs the rough drawing, which is only four or five inches in diameter, with the words "Rat, 1931." He straightens when he hears a couple of students walking through the courtyard. The wide leaves of the mimosa spring back into position and hide his latest creation from curious artists who want to learn something from the great Diego.

THE UMBRELLA

The umbrella held by the umbrella man at Dealy Plaza in 1963 has been a mystery until now. The Zapruder film clearly shows him standing along the route where Kennedy's motorcade was fired upon. A few seconds before the fatal shots, the man opens the umbrella and holds it over his left shoulder. Many conspiracy theorists believe it was the signal to the three shooters. After the President was hit, the umbrella man walked away. The umbrella stayed with him the night he checked out of his Dallas hotel and flew back to Washington. The man used it many times because there was more rain than snow that winter in the nation's capitol. One of his children, about to graduate from college, came home for a holiday and took the umbrella with him when he returned to school. The man never missed it because there were two others in the house. The black umbrella served his son for two years, until the young man's angry live-in girlfriend broke up with him and included the umbrella in a pile of possessions she dumped into her car. She sped away and he never saw her again. Four years later, when she married someone else, she still owned the umbrella. Her new husband took it with him when he was drafted into the Army. This was 1969 and he got sent to Vietnam. Without explaining to his wife, he included the umbrella in his gear because of some notion that it would help against the jungle monsoons. This odd behavior was typical of men who went to Southeast Asia with fear in their hearts. The umbrella didn't make it out of the country, however, because the recruit's drill sergeant found it in his locker. The sergeant screamed that the umbrella would not keep the recruit alive and joyfully twisted the thing in his huge hands. He dropped it on the floor and walked away, leaving the stunned recruit shaking. Then, they all ran out for a drill, so no one saw who picked up the bent umbrella and tossed it in the trash can. That mess made it all the way through the Army base compactors and government trucks that hauled refuse away from major installations. The tons of garbage that held the remains of the umbrella were discarded miles away, at a dump favored by a group of homeless men. They had been collecting odds and ends there for months, and the bent wires and black nylon of what used to be the umbrella were no big deal to the man who plucked them out of the stinking mess. He loved to put things back into working condition, and the umbrella was easy. He even went to the trouble of patching the four holes with some other nylon he had found. Mending the wires was the easy part. Getting the mutilated material to resemble an umbrella was the challenge, but the man was successful enough that when he was arrested in Atlanta, Georgia three months later, the police included an umbrella in the list of marked items belonging to their prisoner. He was charged with aggravated assault and robbery after being caught hitting a liquor store and bashing the clerk with a gun. The umbrella was found in his dirty knapsack, though Atlanta had very little rain that summer. The homeless man's court-appointed public defender had gone to school at The University of Houston, where one of his political science professors was obsessed with the Kennedy assassination. The professor believed it was Fidel Castro all along, though he did allow extensive debate over the theories of CIA involvement. He even showed the Zapruder film, and though there was no discussion of the umbrella man in the class, you can clearly see him down in the bottom left corner of the frame. The homeless man got four years in prison. When he was being processed to be taken away, he asked the public defender to donate his stuff to the nearest homeless shelter. The lawyer gave the man's rags and knapsack to his assistant, a young college student who was repelled by the smelly stuff. Instead of delivering the man's tagged stuff to the special room where they kept such things, she threw everything into the trash. It saved paperwork and, though the assistant didn't know it, gave the next round of homeless men a chance to rehabilitate the ancient umbrella which they found at the same dump site two months later.

THE LAST MAYAN INDIAN

He stands silently on the street corner as many cars go by. Some people wave to him when they recognize him as the last Mayan Indian. Mayans believe in fire clouds. When the world burns, those that are caught standing on busy street corners in major American cities are forgiven and brought back to their people. This last Mayan Indian waves down my cab and hops in. I am the driver and don't know what I am doing picking up someone who looks like him. I turn over my right shoulder and greet him, but he just stares straight ahead. "Where to?" I ask as I head into the busy traffic. He doesn't give me an answer, so I reach the red light on the corner and stop. "Where to?" I turn to him in a panic. I have never had a passenger skip out on a fare, or jump into my cab without saying a word. The last Mayan Indian blinks once, buttons his long trench coat and suddenly jumps out of my cab. "Hey!" I yell, but it is too late, and he has only ridden for one block. Mayans believe that if you touch your sweating chest with a burning ember, you will be able to walk across any bridge and enter the green world with a new face, a purified soul, and be the first ruler of your enemies. I drive home thinking about my brief encounter with the last Mayan Indian. I am very tired and go to sleep when I get to my apartment. I don't even notice the tiny black cross smeared on my forehead. The ashes have not started to turn moist and slowly run down my sleeping face.

THE SPY

The spy wants to reclaim the atomic alphabet the world lost in 1945. He wants to pronounce the atomic language of everything we have been taught to forgive and forget. The spy wanders the desert and comes upon the denial of the rocks. His brother has been an eternal rose since the spy joined the black river—the glowing embers where his secrets suffocate slowly, make him a spy in the theatre of the stone flute—an instrument he claims is silly and sad because it won't blow radioactive dust into the waiting wind. The spy wants to be happy, his estate the wide sky that opens its clouds to anyone skilled at hiding the truth. He crosses in every direction, wrinkles in the brown earth disguised as his dropped soul—hot thoughts he was trained to ignore because they would make him a citizen of the world. When he reaches the Grand Canyon, everything is lost because the open kingdom of red sacrifices is there, its protruding blue drums resembling a line of owls ready to take flight upon the arrival of the spy. This means an encrypted code has finally reached its prehistoric level, dismantling the voices of men who follow the spy into the mossy caverns of their mother's eyes.

circling the tortilla dragon

PART FIVE

NEIL YOUNG

There was an atomic explosion across the white desert and the guy who survived was dressed in a buckskin coat, playing piano in an arroyo. I went to hear him and he handed me his old folk guitar. I strapped it on, noticed the Hendrix button on the strap and wept. He played a few chords on the piano and told me I could join in, on the condition I quit buying bootlegs of his music on the internet. I strummed the guitar, not knowing how to follow the song, but he nodded, his long hair falling over his slumped shoulders. I finally got it and played along as he sang about crossing the border and finding out his woman still loved him. I looked over my shoulder and saw a white electric guitar propped against a boulder. I almost stopped playing, but he shook his head to keep going. He rose from the piano and went to the white guitar, smiled, and strapped it on. I wondered where the amplifier was, because all I could see were rocks, sand, and cactus. He hit the guitar and it twisted into its feedback oath, familiar thundering waves shaking my heart. I wanted to stop playing, but he kept shaking his head, the loud notes rising to rid me of my resistance. We jammed and jammed, the arrangements we made with ourselves keeping us going until dawn, when I saw there were people crossing the concrete bridges over the Rio Grande, coming our way.

THE ART INSTITUTE

I am in the surrealist section of the museum staring at paintings by Salvador Dali, Joan Miro, and Pablo Picasso, when a woman with two heads enters the gallery. She is wearing a pink robe and has tiny tricycles for shoes. She rolls across the floor, one head admiring the great paintings, the other scowling as if she wants to go home. There is a couple on the other side of the room, but they are in love and don't seem to notice. I get out of the way as the two-headed woman glides past me into the next gallery, her shaved heads sporting one metal spike each, with the points protruding as if pounded from the inside. I notice Dali's "Giraffe on Fire" painting. I get closer to focus on the giraffe he drew in the background. I squint to make it out, and a yellow spider emerges from the flames on the giraffe, a stream of yellow spiders following the first one. Soon, the entire masterpiece and gallery wall are covered by hundreds of spiders. Where are the museum guards? The lovers are staring at a nude sculpture as I move away from the spiders and go into the next room, where there are more Picassos. I stop in front of "The Fisherman's Wife," an enormous painting of a nude couple and a child reaching for a fish the man has caught. The plaque says Picasso cut the man's arm off in the revised version of the painting on exhibit here. I try to imagine the man's missing arm, when I am pelted with a shower of stinking fish. They come flying out of the ceiling and bounce off me without hurting, until the smooth gallery floor is covered with fish. Why would this fine museum be doing this? I decide to leave, but four museum guards appear out of nowhere to block my path. Before I can protest, they grab me and carry my down the stairs to the next floor. It is the section I hate the most—the medieval weapons exhibit. Three of the guards hold me as the other grabs a long fourteenth century sword and comes at me. I start to scream and the two-headed woman comes to my rescue. As she karate chops all four guards, I hide behind one of the glass cases. I close my eyes and try to catch my breath amidst the chaos. When I open them, the two-headed woman and the guards are nowhere in sight, but one of my students from the university where I teach has appeared. "Are you okay?" he asks me. "They told me upstairs to come get you. It's your turn to read some poems. We have a good crowd, but the reading is running late with everyone waiting for you."

ELEVATOR MAN

Late for a meeting, I get into the elevator and push the eighth floor button. The elevator is lined with mirrors and I watch myself go up. The bell rings on the fourth floor, the doors open and I move aside to let the next person on, but there is no one there. This annoys me and I hit the close button. The elevator hisses shut and proceeds. Before I know what is happening, it passes the eighth floor and stops on the ninth. The doors open to reveal there is no one in the plush hallway. I can't believe it. I'm late, and the elevator is messed up. I consider taking the stairs down, but I want this fancy thing to work. I push the button for the eighth floor. The elevator responds by going down and stopping on the seventh. Angry, I leap into the hallway and search for the stairs. I can't find any exits and every office door I try is locked. I come back to the row of elevators to find mine sitting open, waiting for me. I push another button, wanting the one next to it to open. It does and I step in. Relieved, I hit the eighth floor button. This time, the elevator stops on the eighth floor and I lean toward the doors, but they do not open. After two seconds, panic sets in. The buttons over the doors say I am on the eighth floor where I want to go. I flip open the emergency phone box and the lights go out. I want to scream and I have started to hyperventilate, when the lights come back on. The doors open quietly and I step out onto the sixth floor. This can't be. The red dials in the elevator said eighth floor, but every office on this one starts with the number six. And, of course, every office is closed. I don't even bother to search for the stairs. Despite what has happened, I hit the button on the wall again and get in. I punch the first floor button and wait as the elevator descends. I step into the lobby and go to the information desk. A grumpy looking guard looks up at me from the bank of television monitors behind his desk. "How can I get to the eighth floor?" I ask. "I'm late for a meeting and the elevator won't stop on that floor." He scowls at me and says without emotion, "There is no eighth floor." "What?" I gasp. He sighs loudly. "What office are you looking for?" "Johnson and Shepley, Suite 812." He looks it up in the directory. "Fifth floor, Suite 515." I start to leave, but it hits me and I turn to ask, "If there is no eighth floor, how come the elevator has a button and light for the eighth floor and how come I stopped on the ninth." The guard stands up, his beer belly straining against his blue uniform. "Mister, you must have the wrong building. There are only seven floors in this place." I don't know what to say, so I just hurry back to the elevators. I go into the one I rode earlier and find the buttons only go to seven. I blink at the row of buttons as if I have never been on an elevator before. I hit the fifth floor button and the doors close. I watch the red dial above the door as it reaches the fourth, then accelerates and stops on the eighth floor. The doors open and I lean against the mirrored wall fighting for air, wondering what is going on, as the most beautiful bank of clouds and sky I have ever seen greet me. I move carefully to the edge of the elevator and look down to find the roof of the building is ten feet below me. This means the elevator I am riding is suspended in mid-air. I scream and the elevator drops, crashing onto the roof. I am thrown out the open door. I roll and come to a stop in front of a small shed where former elevator passengers are kept under lock and key. When I wake among them, they sit me up and the lobby guard peers through the barred window. "I told you there were only seven floors here," he says with a grin.

FLAMING SEPTEMBER

I walk into September and everything changes. Green trees burst into yellow and orange, cold air touching my face. I have never wanted September as badly as I did this year. I walk through a city park and pass a large pond full of tall reeds and wildlife. A bright orange bird with a black head darts across the trail and disappears over the water. I notice something floating in the pond and step into swampy muck to pull out an old tennis shoe. I put it in my knapsack, the idea of someone tossing a shoe out here bothering me. I want to enjoy my walk and think about the poems I am going to write in this month of my birth. I come around a thick grove of white pines to find a box kite hanging in the branches. It sways in the gentle breeze, the fragile balsa wood frame torn in several places, its bright paper shredded. I untangle it, wonder why its owner would leave it in the tree. I spread the thin paper open to find the patterns are color photos of The Beatles, the four famous faces printed all over the kite. I have never seen a Beatles kite before. I try to carry the bulky thing, but after several yards, it crumples in my arms and falls to the ground. Feeling guilty, I leave the remains of the kite and walk faster. I keep going, giant oak trees and evergreens darkening the air around me, the constant sound of hidden birds telling me this is September. I pass another curve in the trail, heavy sumac bushes blocking my view as I almost trip over the wheelchair sitting in the middle of the path. I stop and stare at the empty wheelchair. Where is the person who was riding it? How could they have gotten this far into the park? Perhaps, a handicapped person fell out of the chair and rolled into the thick grass. I search nearby trees and bushes, but do not find a soul. The wheelchair sits alone on the trail. I can't decide whether to leave it there, or push it to the parking lot in case its owner might claim it there. If I took the shoe from the swamp, I should do the right thing and take the wheelchair. I can't stand this. I leave it where I found it. Enough is enough. This is my favorite park in my favorite month. I keep going, trying not to think about the empty wheelchair in the middle of nowhere. This is the strangest walk I have ever taken. Then, I notice the sudden absence of birds. The whole area is eerily quiet. In the distance, oncoming rain clouds tell me why. I head for my car as the bright ball of an early autumn sun turns the sky completely red, bouncing its flaming light off the approaching storm. I get in my car, but don't want to drive anywhere. I roll down the window and smell the cool September air. Nothing else happens. This is September and a heavy burden is lifting off my shoulders. I have taken my walk, found an old shoe, a Beatles kite, and a wheelchair. I recognize a familiar cry and a huge cardinal lands in the tree next to the car. Its red body and distinct head flicker in the leaves as it repeats its lovely call. I start the car and open my knapsack on the seat. Grabbing the muddy shoe, I find it is a small size, perhaps a child's. I slowly pull out of the parking lot and toss the shoe out the window.

BUSY

I am busy living in the new millennium. It fits well with the depression I left back in the twentieth century and I am happier now because I am older and fewer birds fly after me. If I could grow a beard and moustache, I would certainly do it. If I could take my time deciding what I think of my country, it would be easier to live here without feeling pressured that I have to have an opinion, cast a vote, or drink bottled water. I am not sure where I am going with this, but it is a fine season for confessing how we made it past the zero hour and absolutely nothing happened. Even the tiny spider crossing the white rug in the living room is going to make it into the first decade of this new awareness, this incredible insight. I don't step on it or call my cats' attention to it because they love to eat spiders. It passes the leg of my sofa and disappears safely. I read in the newspaper about the 20,000 fish that were found dead in the Guadalupe River near San Antonio where I used to live. It turns out it was fire ant mating season and they were busy. After male fire ants mate with the females in mid-air, they die and fall into the river. When wildlife people cut open the dead fish to see what killed them, they found thousands of fire ants in their bellies. The toxic poison of the male fire ants killed the fish after they gorged on the falling insects. I am busy thinking about this because I was attacked by fire ants several times while living in the area. This thought fits with what I was going to say about the end of our beloved century. I have two large windows in my office at home and an old, large desk. When I open any book from my office shelves, I always use both hands.

MAN ON THE WALL

I stood in front of the old house that used to belong to my grandmother and did not want to see it again, because I was born there. I had returned to my hometown for my father's funeral and been drawn to this neighborhood. I decided to leave without approaching the house and took a short cut through the alley across the street. As I turned into it, there was a man sitting quietly on a high, adobe wall that bordered the alley, his legs hanging over the ledge. He looked down at me and I looked up at him, but we did not say a word to each other. He was dressed in dirty work clothes like he had been painting a house or digging trenches somewhere. He wore an old baseball hat that shaded his eyes from me. I noticed that he had a long nose and a ragged beard, as if he had not shaved in days. As I started to move on, his left leg rose swiftly like he didn't want me to leave. I paused. "What do you want?" I asked. His friendly grin showed yellow teeth with gaps. He didn't say a word, but pointed down the alley. I decided he was a neighborhood drunk in search of his next bottle and kept going. I managed to move about ten feet when I saw what he had been pointing at. My path down the alley was blocked by another wall that had not been there minutes before. Startled, I turned and breathed a sigh of relief when I saw that the entry to the alley where I had come in was open. The man on the wall watched me, his hands folded peacefully in his lap, his blue workshirt spotted with sweat stains. I had been down this alley before and the barrier had never been there. I returned to the man on the wall. "What is going on?" I asked him. "Who are you?" From his perch above my head, the man yawned without answering and waited for my next move. I started toward the street where I had come from, but found I could not leave the alley. Something made me stop at its entrance. My grandmother's house sat decaying across the street, and the dirt lot next door, where I played as a boy, was overrun by weeds. I returned to the man on the wall. This time, he spoke first. "You are Fernando's son. I remember you." He said this with regret. For the first time, his dark eyes under the baseball cap lit up. "Why are you passing through here? Doña Julia's house is over there." He pointed to my grandmother's house, neither one of us mentioning the fact she had been dead for over ten years and my father had just passed away. "I wanted to see it one more time," I answered. "How do you know my father and grandmother?" The stranger smiled again. "Because I have been up here for a long time," he told me. I didn't know what he meant, but I noticed that the wall blocking my path to the bus stop was now gone. I realized I was losing it, and my return was causing paranoia. "Why have you been sitting up there?" I asked him. "Please tell me your name." He swung one leg over the other and sighed. "I have been sitting on this wall for a long time and have seen many boys like you come home and visit. But, you never stay. When you return, you walk right past me. You are one of the few who has talked to me." I didn't want to hear anymore. Without saying goodbye, I bolted down the alley. I ran and barely made it in time to hop on the bus. As I pulled myself up the steps and fumbled for change, I thought I saw the man standing on the corner as if he had finally come down from his wall to see me get on the bus. I paid the driver and moved to the back seats. The bus turned the corner, but it was enough time for me to look up the street. There was no one on the corner.

JOEY'S DIABLO

Joey's Diablo appeared on the corner of Frutas and Alameda one night. The dudes called him Joey's Diablo because Joey had been the first to spot him pitching pennies in the alley behind Toro's Bar. When Joey stepped forward to toss coins with the dark figure, it grinned at Joey, then disappeared. He told Frankie and Saul the thing in the alley had red horns, a red face, and a tail it tried to hide under a black raincoat. The second time, Saul saw the Diablo leaning against the telephone pole and cried, "Hey! It's Joey's Diablo! It's Joey's Diablo!" Frankie, Joey, and Luis came running, but stopped behind a parked car, none of them wanting to get close to the Diablo, which was dressed in black leather pants and a Tupac Shakur t-shirt, its bright red tail tied like a belt around its waist. The Diablo's wicked grin illuminated the gloomy corner as it waved to them with a long finger to come closer. When the dudes got a good look at the horns on its head and caught the smell of sulfur, Frankie and Luis ran away. Joey and Saul stood their ground. "Maybe we should get out of here," Saul whispered to Joey, who stared at the Diablo. "No, man," Joey answered, "I'm going to talk to the bro' and find out what he wants." Saul couldn't believe his friend was going to get closer to the evil-looking thing. As Joey took a step, the boys were blinded by a light that popped out of the alley. Saul ran away, the last thing he saw through watery eyes making him run faster—the Diablo had his arm around Joey's shoulders and was whispering in the boy's ear. Joey rubbed his stunned face and listened to the Diablo. "Hey, Joey boy. How's it going, man? I know you're cool, so I wanted to drop by and see you. It looks like you're the one with the huevos to hang with me." Joey almost gagged at the smell of reptilian death as the Diablo pressed his face closer to Joey's sweating cheeks. "Listen, Joey. I gotta deal for you." The Diablo hissed through his nose, his tail uncurling to rub Joey's leg. Joey wanted to run from this, but was held there by the Diablo's arm around his shoulders. "Joey, my man. Here it is," the Diablo began as the street emptied of dudes and cruising cars. "This is what I want you to do. Take this gun, go home, and shoot your old man through the head. He's drunk and passed out. We know he's beating the shit out of your mama and putting the meat to Loncha down the street. Guys like you believe in justice, so doing your old man will settle it. Then you and I can move up from making pennies on these streets. You dig?" Joey stared at his Diablo who had just described exactly what was happening at home. He took the cold Saturday night special from the greasy fingers of his Diablo and turned away without a word. Joey crossed the dark corners where his friends hung out till four in the morning, but they weren't there. His house was two blocks away. Joey could hear the crunching of broken beer glass under his Reeboks as he neared it. The gun felt heavy in his hand as he climbed the porch of his home, lights off inside. He paused by the door and set the gun on the torn seat of the porch swing. He couldn't do this. He backed off from the gun and got a good view of his father's open bedroom window. Rolando's drinking bouts often ended in him punching Sandra, Joey's mother, before passing out. Rolando had never touched Joey, who always avoided his father. Now he wanted to run back to his Diablo and tell it to leave him alone, but the window changed his mind. Joey grabbed the gun, went to the open screen and peered inside. His father snored on his bed, Joey's mother always sleeping in another room. Knowing the old man was out cold, Joey pulled the screen off and climbed inside. He saw the flash from the alley again, blinded by balls of light in his eyes as he went up to Rolando. He blinked, wanting to shoot the wall or his old man's stinking clothes on the floor, but he fired two shots into his father, one in the back and one in the head. The explosions lit up the room and Joey heard his mother scream down the hallway. Gripping the hot pistol, Joey leaped out the window and ran down the street, Poncho's dogs next door barking like crazy, a few lights coming on in the desperate neighborhood, but no one came out as he sprinted to the alley where his Diablo was waiting. The creature's smile lit up the night like the echoes of gunfire that rang in Joey's ears. He tucked the gun in his belt, bent over and tried to catch his breath, then felt his Diablo come closer. The cold hand with long fingernails brushed his back. "Good job, Joey," his Diablo whispered. "Congratulations. Your bro's will be proud of you." Joey straightened when he thought he heard sirens in the distance. There was no one around except him and his Diablo. Joey felt the hot steel of the gun against his waist and pulled it fast. He aimed at his Diablo, surprising the ugly thing. "Fuck you," Joey said. "You talk about my bro's and bring them into this and you're dead. This is just between me and my old man." The Diablo floated a few feet off the ground, the grin turning into a sneer Joey didn't like. "Hey Joey, my man. I told you we are moving up and you did the right thing. Be cool. Be cool. You know nobody around here cares about your old man." Those were the Diablo's last words as Joey pumped four bullets into him, their force spinning the Diablo several times, the dirt and tin cans in the alley swirling in a wind the thing called up as it flew away, red human blood splattered all over the asphalt, both entrances to the alley suddenly blocked off by police cars, their lights flashing redder than Joey's Diablo.

THE CHRISTMAS GIFT

Elizondo Robles got the package two days before
Christmas. He was surprised that Luna Corrales, his old girlfriend,
had sent it. They had broken up one year ago, after she caught him
with Linda. Luna's gift was a large, square box about three feet deep
wrapped in bright red foil. Elizondo set it on his desk and opened it
without trouble. The inside held a similar, smaller box wrapped in
bright green foil—this was big time giving. Inside this one, he found
a piñata of a donkey with a card that said, "Break me open!" Elizondo
laughed because Luna loved jokes like this. He took a hammer from
his work bench and smashed the papier mache burro. Out spilled a
smaller box wrapped in bright blue foil. He tore it open to find an
old pair of his boxer shorts, which he had forgotten he had, the patterns of Goofy the cartoon dog recalling that first night at Linda's.
How did Luna get her hands on these? Inside his enormous boxers,
he found a smaller box wrapped in bright orange foil. This one was
more like a package, oval and somewhat flattened. He cut it open
and stared at a pack of store-bought tortillas, the old things growing
mold around the edges, giving off a foul smell, one end of the bag cut
open to hold a small thing wrapped in bright purple foil. By this time,
Elizondo had lost his sense of humor. He took a breath and clipped
the tape off the purple foil. The cassette tape inside had a sticker that
said, 'Play side A at once!" He went to his stereo, popped the thing
in and stood before his speakers as Luna's sweet voice came on, "Hey,
baby, Merry Christmas! (short giggle with what sounded like a man's
voice in the background). If you are playing this, you must have
loved the tortillas, sweetie. Guess where I am with all my clothes off
as I tape this? (more giggles and the sound of sipping liquid). Hey,
Eli baby. I just wanted to wish you a happy holiday and remind you

that there is one more gift. Don't think my little naked voice is all there is. Bye baby!" A sudden click. Elizondo stared at his stereo as a long hiss followed. He stopped the tape and went to the first box, the one in red. It was large and empty, each layer of surprises inside it having led him to the tape, but Luna said there was one more gift. He didn't have much time to think about it, however, because the outer box started to move, shaking on the desk as if some live thing had been overlooked inside. Elizondo grabbed the hammer and pushed the large box onto its side. Pieces of red foil fell off as the cardboard expanded and a life-sized blow-up doll with an uncanny resemblance to Linda emerged, its huge pink breasts and dark hole smiling at Elizondo through shreds of foil. He had screwed Linda three times, then kicked her out of his life after Luna caught them. He had not seen her in almost a year. The doll hissed and grew larger, its ballooning size pushing it off the desk as it started to fill the room. Elizondo moved out of the way as the distorted thing came at him, the colored holiday foils sticking to her hard nipples, the tortillas smashed under her floating body, Elizondo trying to puncture it with the hammer, but having no luck. He was furious. As the doll rolled toward his Christmas tree with the fancy lights, he was afraid it would knock it over, but then it occurred to him that the hot bulbs might burst the doll. He huddled behind the desk as the naked Linda smashed into the Christmas tree. A whoosh and sudden pop mushroomed through the room, the doll exploding into a million pieces, with tree, lights, cords, and tortillas flying like shrapnel. Elizondo heard a slapping sound. As he opened his eyes, he received the final surprise—dozens of condoms in their wrappers raining on his head, the doll having carried them inside as the last gift for a cool dude who loved to open packages this time of year.

Tia Anselma's prediction came true when the tumbleweeds, bunched by the desert wind against the house, started to explode into clouds of dust. The entire family came running outside as they heard random pops and bursts. There were at least a dozen dry, brown tumbleweeds piled atop one another, and each exploded. Tia Anselma held her hands against her open mouth, her eyes bulging, until she caught her breath and yelled that she knew this would happen. It meant the heaviest dust storm in years was about to blow through town. It began with a darkening sky that turned light brown, the first tumbleweeds rolling down the street like wheels from nowhere. The air was heavy with dirt and stinging particles that burned their eyes. Tia Anselma led her family back onto the porch and they stood watching from inside the screened door as the accelerating race of tumbleweeds flew by. Small dark brown ones shot down the street like basketballs. Two giant ones cleared paths on the dirt street by collecting everything like magnets. By the time they bounced from right to left in front of the house, newspapers, toilet paper, even diapers from Maria's clothesline had joined the sticky, growing mass. Tia Anselma rubbed her eyes and made her nieces and nephews go inside and close the main door as the dust storm howled and shut out the afternoon sun. She could not see anything in the brown fog except the mounting pile of tumbleweeds. Dozens of them were stuck on the fenceposts in the yard and more were piling up on the sidewalk and blocking the porch steps. Tia Anselma was starting to panic, because she knew what drowning in thousands of tumbleweeds would mean. The wind howled louder as she opened the door. It slammed back against her as dust flew into the front room. She tried to force the screen door open, but it was blocked by a four-foot-high mass of tumbleweeds. She pushed and pushed at the door as weeds popped and snapped before her. She felt their thorns on her bare arms, her long black hair swirling across her eyes, blinding her but protecting her against the stinging dust. She heard the kids yell something as the wind lifted her dress. She kicked out with her sandals and demolished two more weeds in her path. They were instantly replaced by four more that flew across the yard and hit Tia Anselma in the chest and head. She stumbled back and fell into the pile. She could hear her nieces and nephews shouting inside the house as she was carried along the porch by the wind. She reached a pillar and held on, tried to get to her feet, her dress twisted around her head, and managed to stand up just as a bright yellow weed flew over her. She ducked, and then she thought she heard breaking glass. She let go of the pillar, trying to reach the door, and joined the dust storm. She screamed louder than the wind as it carried her off the porch, lifted her three feet off the ground, and carried her across the yards of two other houses which, remarkably, had only three or four tumbleweeds stuck in them. Only Tia Anselma's house was surrounded by hundreds. She landed hard near Al's porch and passed out, her dress protecting her face and head. When she felt someone nudge her shoulder, she awoke to an incredible stillness. Al helped her to her feet and they stared at her house. It was completely covered by enormous mounds and clusters of bright green bushes, blossoming plants, and colorful flowers. They camouflaged the house all the way to the roof. Her five nieces and nephews played in the bright afternoon sun, the youngest boy calmly watering the plants with the garden hose. Tia Anselma rubbed the dozens of red scratches on her bare arms and cried and cried, her howling reminding Al of the storm that had just passed.

FROGS

Benny lay in bed and listened to the thunderstorm over his house. The raindrops fell at a steady rate as he turned to the window and watched lightning bolts streak across the sky. He opened the glass, breathed cool night air, and waited for the frogs. Benny believed the frogs would return because of his dream a few nights ago. In it the frogs came back after a rain, because they always got lost after storms and wanted help from boys like Benny. They had to find the pond where their families were waiting for them to return. The frogs repeated the chant, "Not here. Not here. Not here," over and over in the dream. He opened his eyes now and three frogs sat croaking on the bed, their throats bubbling wide. When he sat up, the frogs sprang off the bed. He wanted to ask them if they were lost, but didn't know how to talk to them. He wondered if he could help them get back to their pond. He was familiar with the streams that ran behind his house, the wooded hills leading down to the freeway a couple of miles away. It was the area where Benny played alone, his sanctuary of rocks and cottonwoods. He removed the window screen and the three frogs sprang out. Benny dressed and went outside, knowing these frogs were the ones in his dream. He couldn't see them in the night shadows, but knew they would be headed toward the stream that ran near the house, so he followed the sound of water and came upon the sloping bank. He heard splashing, and then he skidded down the slippery grass to the edge of the water. Despite the moonless night, he could make out hundreds of frogs jumping and flying over the stream. They were all moving in the same direction and Benny followed them. He struggled to climb the opposite bank, and when he got to the top he witnessed something he had never seen before—frogs swarming over themselves to climb a cottonwood tree that sagged against a mound of rocks, its gray limbs and trunk turning green from the mass of frogs. Its branches were covered with the squirming things, many of them falling, to be replaced by hundreds more, until the cottonwood was completely covered with a bubbling layer of frogs, their croaking a deafening roar. Then the swarm of frogs stopped croaking all at once. In the deep silence, Benny heard the snapping of wood. The tree bent closer to the pile of rocks behind it, dislodged some boulders with its frog-coated branches, then came down in a crash. A wave of frogs jumped off it and hit the water, many disappearing downstream. Benny ran down the bank, slipped, and fell in. He splashed about on all fours as the mud and frogs covered his body, keeping him from standing in the shallow mess. Benny panicked as his arms and legs were weighed down by the frogs. Dozens hit his back and head as they skipped away. Covered in slime, he managed to crawl back to the bank and pull himself out, to lie gasping on the grass as more frogs used his wet body as a springboard to the darkness. He lay back and let it happen, until the pounding of the frogs sent him into a deep sleep. He woke in the morning to the sound of his parents calling his name. Benny sat up and pulled his sore legs out of the water. The morning sun came over the high bank and blinded him for an instant, then his father appeared on the other side. "Benny! Where the hell have you been?" His father climbed down the bank to retrieve his son. As he pulled him up by the arms, Benny noticed the dead frogs. Hundreds of them floated belly-up in the motionless water. He tried to point this out to his father, but his father grabbed him roughly and pushed him toward home, angry at how long it had taken to find him. At the top of the bank, before his father blocked his view, Benny looked back across the stream. The cottonwood stood tall and unbroken above the rocks piled perfectly around it. As his father shoved him toward the house, Benny had one last view of the green water full of dead frogs.

Sonny refused to get rid of the rusting remains of his wrecked '56 Chevy. It sat in the front yard of his house for eight years, tall grass growing inside the windowless frame as it sank into the earth. One day, Freddy knocked on Sonny's door to ask if he could take the hood off the car and use it for a sculpture he wanted to make. Sonny couldn't believe Freddy wanted to take his car apart. Freddy was a crazy artist, but this was too much. "Sculpture?" Sonny asked in disbelief. "What does my car have to do with your art?" Freddy was patient because he had not told Sonny everything. Sonny didn't know that Freddy and his artist friend, Tencho, had been secretly stealing parts off the car for weeks. They had challenged each other to come up with the most outrageous metal sculptures out of stolen junk from Sonny. Freddy had even invested in blowtorches and fuel tanks for the project. Tencho would come over and they'd work in Freddy's garage. "Come on, Sonny," Freddy pleaded. "It's only junk. I'm doing you a favor by taking the thing out of your yard. It's ugly out there." "No!" Sonny yelled at him. "It's mine. That car means a lot to me. You don't know what that car was before I retired it." "Retired it?" Freddy snickered. "Didn't you get drunk and crash right through Mona's bakery?" Sonny glared at him, "You little creep. I had the best wheels in town for years. That car could outrace anybody. You don't know how many drag races I won out on Western Highway. I retired undefeated." Freddy shook his head. It was no use. He would have to take parts of Sonny's car without telling him. He waved goodbye and waited for nightfall to make his move, this time without Tencho. When he noticed the lights were out in Sonny's house, he figured Sonny had gone to bed because his regular car, a '98 Ford pick-up, was in the driveway. Freddy crept through the tall, uncut grass in the yard and hid alongside the hood. Many of the engine parts were long gone, but Freddy knew the radiator was intact. It was going to be the chest and shoulders of the metal man he was sculpting. He rose in the moonlight and carefully began to lift the broken hood. It yawned with a metallic screech, and Freddy paused, holding the heavy thing half open. No lights came on in the house, so he kept lifting and was surprised to find the rusting bar that held the hood up was still there. He pulled the bar up and set the open hood on it. He grabbed his wrenches and struggled with the rusted bolts on the radiator. He got one of them off and was straining against the next when the upraised hood caved in, its weight crushing Freddy's skull and killing him instantly. His body muted the noise of the thing slamming shut. Sonny, who was a deep sleeper, never heard the commotion. When he came out in the morning to fetch the newspaper, Sonny calmly gazed at a pair of legs sticking out from the junk. He called the cops and an ambulance. Freddy was pronounced dead, and Sonny had to file a report about his friend, the artist who died trying to steal parts from Sonny's beloved car. As a result of the accident, Sonny had the car towed to a junkyard and got forty dollars for it. Two weeks later, his six-year old daughter, Nenny, was running across the yard and fell on the spot where the car used to be, cutting her chin open on a sliver of metal hiding in the grass. One month later, a huge pool of oil seeped out of the ground and soaked the grass, even though there was nothing left of the car. One week passed and Sonny woke in the night to a fire in his front yard. The next morning a perfect circle of scorched grass and ash had replaced the oil. Two weeks later, a gas leak blew Sonny's house to smithereens, but it was a weekday and no one was home. Sonny and his wife built a new house on the site. He was the owner of a used car lot and collected the wrecked remains of two more Chevys in his front yard over the next five years, but no grass would grow in the dirt yard of his new home.

Manny loved to collect colored stones and had shoeboxes full of the smoothest and most colorful stones his friends had ever seen. He picked up stones on his lone walks, the best hunting ground for beautiful stones being the arroyo by the irrigation canal where he found rocks he had not seen before. His favorites included a black stone with a tiny hole eroded in its center. He would hold it to the light, squint through the hole, and see something different each time. The shapes of light that flew through the stone amazed him. They were followed by images of stained glass windows, kaleidoscope designs, even patterns of orange and red birds. He saw things like that when he squinted through the hole. He wanted to fill the two glass jars his mother had bought him. It had taken some convincing, but she finally got them for what she called his "rock collection." Manny shook his head and corrected her. "Stones, Mama. They are stones." The day after getting the glass jars, Manny went on his hiking adventure full of excitement. The irrigation canal was at a low level, so he would find hundreds of stones washed into it. Low water meant erosion in the arroyo would be extensive—fresh soil settling in its bottom. He chose to look there first and splashed waist deep in the arroyo, something his mother had warned him not to do. Even though farm fields lay nearby, the uncultivated stretch of desert along their borders was full of deep holes and hidden dangers. Manny bent down and scooped up fresh smelling mud with the metal pan he carried. Twigs, big rocks, and a few dull colored stones came up. He dumped them and clouds of mud spread around his bare legs. He wiped his muddy hands on his shorts and stepped forward gingerly. He brought up another panful and found three beautiful stones. The first was an egg-shaped white one with brown veins through it. He pocketed it and plucked the second stone from the pan—a round gray with deep red circles. As he held it to the sun, it reflected light. The third stone in the pan was the real find—its transparent green, honey residue glowed in the sunlight like a magic lantern. In his excitement, he put both stones into the pan and moved a few more feet through the brown water. As he slipped, he knew he should have put all three in his pocket right away and examined them on dry ground. He fell face first into the muck and as the pan hit the water with a plop, he went under. When he surfaced in the three-foot-deep mess, the empty pan was floating nearby. In anger, he splashed the water with it, hurtling more mud on his head. Manny climbed out onto the low cement wall of the irrigation canal and wiped the mud from his stinging eyes. He remembered the white stone and reached into his pocket, but he felt an odd shape there. He pulled a plastic toy soldier out of his soaked pants pocket. He held the kneeling rifleman in one hand and dug deeper into the pocket with the other. No white stone. Manny couldn't recall putting the plastic figure in his pocket. He had quit playing with Army men years ago. He studied the three-inch green soldier and noticed grains of white and brown smeared over it. The hot summer sun was already drying his clothes as he left. He hopped over the iron barrier near the irrigation gate and threw the toy soldier into the clear flow of the canal. He thought for a moment about the green stone that had lit up his pan, and then he hurried home, already planning which of the stones in his shoeboxes would be the first to go into the glass jars.

circling the tortilla dragon

PART SIX

MY FIRST GIRLFRIEND

My first girlfriend walks down the street. I have not seen her since high school thirty years ago, but she looks the same and has not aged one bit. Her long blonde hair and hippie clothes are bright against the morning light that breaks through the trees. We stop on the sidewalk as we recognize each other, though it is obvious I have gotten old. "Hi. How have you been?" she asks without surprise and gives me a great smile. I don't know what to say. I swallow. "Uh, okay. Where have you been?" I shake my head like it is the wrong thing to say. She gives me an expression that says I'm a jerk and this is why she gave up on me years ago. "What do you mean, where have I been?" she replies. I don't know what to say. She cuts the awkward silence by stepping up to me and giving me a kind kiss on the cheek. I can smell the hippie musk on her body, fresh as it was the last time we were together three decades ago. She doesn't say goodbye as she goes on her way. I stand there with my hands in my pockets, this time warp forgotten by the thick knot of pain in my heart. I try to forget what just happened before I reach my place of business and open it for the day. The neon sign over the building says "Girls! Girls! Girls," but I have not turned it on yet. Inside my club, there are blonde girls everywhere, their clothes on. Their wavy blonde hair adds various shades of light to the quiet club as they sit at the tables and smoke cigarettes, gossip, and wait for their big boss to light things up.

BLUE BUTTERFLIES

It happens again. He gets a package in the mail containing six blue butterflies expertly mounted in a smooth wooden box with a glass lid. Each beautiful butterfly is five inches wide with open wings. It is the third box he has received and he does not know who is sending them. There is no return address on the package and the mailman does not know anything about them. He sets the box down next to the other two on his desk. Now he has three boxes with a total of eighteen bright blue butterflies. He has not lifted the glass off any of them, afraid they will disintegrate. He bends close to his desk lamp and sees that this box contains six butterflies different than the first two sets. Holding the glass to the light, he reads, "Made by your father" in black print on the left wing of each butterfly. It is like someone typed the words in a small font on a computer, then pasted them on the wings. He sets the box down and thinks about this because his father has been dead for six years. He picks up the other cases of butterflies and inspects them carefully under the light. There are no words on any of the sheer blue wings of these earlier sets. He wants to call his mother, who lives in another city, and ask her about the butterflies, but he's had a difficult time getting along with her since his father died. Instead, he crosses the hall of his apartment and quietly enters the bedroom where his new girlfriend, a brunette he met only two weeks ago, is sleeping. He nudges her naked shoulder and she wakes in a fog. "Come look at what came in the mail," he whispers as she sits up, rubbing her sleepy eyes. He has hidden the butterfly boxes each time she has spent the night and has never mentioned them before. This morning he felt like taking them out, and then the third one showed up. His girlfriend follows him into his study and yawns as he holds up the new set of blue butterflies. "Oh,

I didn't know you were a collector," she says when she sees what they are. "I'm not," he answers impatiently. "I have no idea who sent these to me. Look at the wings." His girlfriend squints closer and reads, "Made by your father." Her eyes grow large and she jumps back. "Oh, my God!" she cries out. "What is it?" he asks, now frightened. "I can't believe it," she gasps and runs to the bedroom. For one instant, he delights in seeing her naked beauty, then follows her into the bedroom to find her pulling her panties on. "What is it?" She is frightened. "You fool!" she answers. "You've always been so busy with your face down there, that you haven't even noticed." She picks up her bra and holds her left arm straight over her head. "Take a look at this," she commands. He comes closer in the dim light of the room and makes out the blue butterfly tattooed in her armpit. Right under the butterfly, also in blue, are the words, "Made by your father."

THE GLASS EYE

Folio had a glass eye he loved to bounce on the floor. It would bounce higher than a basketball. He would sit on the sofa and bounce it. It would almost touch the light on the ceiling before coming down into his open hand. One day, as he was bouncing his glass eye, he heard a knock on the door. He quickly screwed the eye into his left socket and went to the door. When he opened it, he met a tall, thin woman who wore nothing but a yellow bikini. Folio blinked several times because the late fall air was chilly and he wondered how she could stand there like that. The woman had brown hair and a deep tan. She smiled at him without saying a word. Folio was not good with women, so he just stood there in his old sweater and sweatpants and stared. The woman's body reflected the cold, goose bumps all over her exposed skin. Folio stared at her small, yet dominant breasts and her flat belly. She stood barefoot on the cold cement of the porch. Folio didn't know what to do. He was captivated by her sweet smile and red lips. He noticed she held both hands behind her back, which helped her breasts reach closer to him. She extended her right hand to him. It held a tiny, white box. He took it from her tiny hand. Before he could look at her body again, the woman in the yellow bikini turned and ran from the porch. Folio panicked, but could not move. He thought he saw her get in a waiting van. He quickly shut the door. His old slippers scraped on the wooden floor as he went back to his trusted sofa. He sat down and carefully opened the tiny box. A glass eye stared up at him. It's eyeball was green. Folio's real eye and his artificial one were brown. He took the new eye and held it up to the light. He removed his left eye with a quick pinch of his fingers, then inserted the new one. He turned to the window beside the sofa and saw a woman standing outside, her face pressed to the glass. He rose, blinked, and realized it was the woman in the yellow bikini. Now she was enormously fat and her breasts were huge. Folds of fat skin drew him to the window. It was the same woman. She smiled at him and pointed to the door. Folio almost tripped on his untied slippers as he ran to it. He swung the door open and the fat woman flew into his arms. As they hugged, Folio's artificial eye flew out of his hand and bounced loudly across the floor. He tried to turn, but the perfumed body of the huge woman kept him from seeing where the eye landed. They pushed each other toward the sofa and Folio heard the glass eye roll off into the hidden shadows of his living room.

THE GHOST

The ghost bothered Tony for a few weeks, then disappeared. Tony noticed the man behind him when he was shaving in the bathroom one morning. Lather on his face, Tony turned to his right as the figure stood in the bathroom door. He thought he saw a man there, but didn't find anyone when he turned. Later that week, Tony saw a man sitting at his kitchen table. Tony had just returned from his daily jog and was dripping sweat. He went to the refrigerator for his Gatorade and was wiping his face with a towel when he spotted the man at the table. Tony jumped, and the man, who wore a white beard, vanished. Tony carefully walked over to where the man had been sitting. There was a ring of water from the bottom of a glass on the tabletop. Tony wanted to tell his friends about this, but was afraid they would think he was crazy or having a flashback. After all, he had done lots of drugs in college. He tried to forget what he had seen. Ten days later, the man appeared while Tony was fucking a woman he had met at work. He had been trying for weeks to get her to go out with him. As they heaved and pumped on the bed, Tony felt someone press a hand on his ass. At first he thought he was fucking too hard, but then he felt the cold fingers creep farther down his ass. He pulled out suddenly and the woman screamed. Tony jumped up, his red dick throbbing in the air. He turned and recognized the man who stood at the foot of the bed. Then his father, who had been dead for eight years, disappeared before his eyes. Tony collapsed on the floor. The woman sat up and glared at Tony, whose tool was quickly fading between his legs. Her look of outrage told him it was over. She dressed and left without a word. Tony managed to fall asleep a couple of hours later. In the morning, he found another ring of water on the table. He didn't wipe it with a towel as he had done the first time. He let it dry into the wood instead, and never saw the ghost again.

THIRTY SIX ROOMS

In each of the thirty-six rooms, you will find a man and woman making love. There are only two of them, but they inhabit thirty-six rooms. There is only one bed in the house, but the couple are making love in each room—their entwined, sweating bodies reflected in the multiple walls and moans of the tired house. In the thirty-six rooms, you will find a man and woman wishing they were not themselves, each holding onto their secret thoughts without knowing they are exactly the same. When the woman comes, several of her selves disappear for a moment in some of the rooms. When she relaxes, she is everywhere again. When the man comes, he tries to be more than thirty-six men, but his energy is spent and he can't fill any more rooms. When he relaxes, he is the only man the woman thinks about. In the thirty-six rooms, you will find necessary peace—a source of energy from the two of them having loved each other through the years of joy and pain. In the rooms, you will see a woman and man rising and the woman showering first. When she is done, she goes to bed naked and does not wait for the man to finish his shower. He takes his time in the steam of the bathroom. When he gets ready for bed, she is already asleep. In the thirty-six rooms, you will find a man and woman loving each other, their separate dreams separating the walls and doors of the magnificent house, until the first sense of morning wakes them to hold each other again.

HOBBIES

The marbles hit the bucket of water, splash drops onto the mirror that is tied to the bucket handle which reflects light from the sun toward the waiting match stick. The stick is tied by a string to an open window and lies against a ball of cotton. When the reflected light ignites the match, the flames burn the cotton. The fire races up the curtain and spreads throughout the room, the smoke and burning walls making the couple who live in the house panic and run outside, where they stumble over the hoses of the fire department. The young man and woman who trip and fall are wearing summer shorts and roll with their legs in the air, exposing private parts of themselves to one fireman who has healthy fantasies in his mind. While fighting the fire, he thinks about the man and woman naked with him watching. Before he can come out of his fantasy, a second fireman pulls on the hose and it goes flying out of the first one's dreaming hands. The powerful jet of water sends the hose into the windshield of a police car and the shattered glass flies everywhere. One splinter lands in the evergreen tree of the yard and is caught in the branches. The sliver of glass stays in the tree for months until autumn arrives, then a squirrel chasing a second squirrel down the tree gets the sliver of glass caught in its front right paw. The squirrel does not know what this pain is about and flies out of the tree. The pet mongrel dog, unhappy about being out in the oncoming frost, grabs the squirrel in mid-air. It tears it to pieces and the sliver of glass in the squirrel's paw gets caught in the throat of the dog. It runs in painful circles, howling and howling. The couple, who moved back into the house only four weeks ago, are woken from their afternoon nap by their suffering dog. They bound into their clothes, leap off the waving waterbed and go to the window. The fireman who started all this clicks the camera off and puts it in his bag, zips his pants up, and waves goodbye to the couple who are leaning out the window, calling the bloody dog who won't stop howling. Across the street, a boy sits on his front porch steps and watches the spinning dog. The boy puts his box of matches away, stuffs the cotton balls into his pocket and goes inside to look for his cat.

THEY'VE JUST BEEN FED

A man and his dog go for a walk on the first day after the new millennium. The park is cold and empty, and the few people who pass the man and dog don't look up from their bundled coats. The man walks his dog every day of the year, but the new century is different. As the man pulls on the leash and the dog stops, he makes sure no one is around, then takes a piece of gum out of his coat pocket and puts it in the dog's mouth. The animal, a small collie, loves the gum and chews it for a few seconds, swallowing it as any dog would. The man smiles at this and they continue their outing. A few yards down the cement path, the man spots a city trash can—a black one reinforced with an iron grill and chained to the sidewalk. The dog wags his tail and pulls on the leash, but the man takes his time digging into the overflowing trash. The smell doesn't bother him as his arm sinks deeper into the mess, until his hand feels something. He pulls out a wooden ice cream stick, which makes him very happy. The cold January of the new century has frozen the remains of the chocolate and vanilla bar to the stick. The man pulls on the leash to calm his dog down and licks the stick. In the cold, it makes his tongue hurt, but the taste of the leftover ice cream is what he loves. He starts to walk again, the stick protruding out of his mouth, one drop of chocolate falling off to land on his clean, white shirt, missing the tie and the flashy business suit he wears every day. When the dog and man come to a busy intersection at the end of the park, they wait for the light to turn. When it flashes to green, the dog hops forward. The man looks both ways and barely notices the morning traffic, which has stopped for the red light. Halfway across the street, the man spits the ice cream stick out of his mouth. It bounces on the asphalt, flips toward the curb, then lands on the freshly shined shoe of another man on his way to work. The man with the dog does not see this, but picks up the pace because his high-rise apartment is one block away and he needs to drop the dog off and get to his office. He has already passed by when the second man looks down, sees the wet ice-cream stick on his shoe, and bends to retrieve it. He holds it gingerly between two fingers. Other people waiting to cross don't notice as the man hesitates, then places the stick in his mouth. He moves it around with his tongue as the red light turns green and he casually crosses, thinking about the day's work ahead.

circling the tortilla dragon

I QUIT EATING

I quit eating beans and tortillas. I smiled, and quit. I've killed the spirit of those foods by being myself. So that I can tell the truth, I have stopped depending on such common foods to keep me going. I hope you believe me. My mind is clearer when I open cans of tuna and salmon and bite into my wheat bread. It is a new life. Even the jalapenos I refuse to give up sting my throat with more power, since I gave up beans and tortillas. You can say goodbye to these things and never regret it. Walk backwards and touch the hot stove with your back. It is warm, but it will not feed you with the things you have desired your entire life. Men play guitars in other rooms. Women I love disappear from my dreams. Dogs bark outside the door, and my cats run guiltily across my clean kitchen table. There is a time to feel hungry and a time to be full. I even have better dreams since giving up the food of my birth. I run to work, don't walk anymore. You might wonder what happened to make me change what I eat. My big stomach is changing, fading, growing thinner, even the color of my skin is changing—something I thought I would never admit. I quit eating beans and tortillas. One of my dreams gave me the reason for quitting—the last troubling dream I had before giving up the food. I dreamed I was a stalk of corn growing in a corn-field somewhere in the Southwest. There is nothing wrong with this, but I saw the migrant workers picking the fields and harvesting the corn. They burned and sweated in the hot sun all day. It took them several days to reach the row where I grew. All this happened in my dream. I waited to be harvested, but when they got to my row, they skipped me. My corn was ready, large, and the same quality as the tons they carried away. Yet, it was left to rot in the field. I woke up when my stalk and cob shriveled to nothing. I quit eating beans and tortillas because that dying plant made its way back into the soil and told me I had been wrong my entire life. I quit eating the things my mother and grandmother raised me on because I could not depend on such nourishing things any longer. The harvest was over. I quit eating beans and tortillas to emerge from my body and be able to dream about a harvested field where any worker can find me and accept me as part of the crop. This is the only way to be myself, the pure act of appetite, hunger, and resolve. I will not eat another bean or taste the luscious power of a warm tortilla ever again because I have left the kitchen of my home for good. I will find new food, new ways of cooking, new habits to enrich my body without harm, without that dream of being left alone in the field. If you are not sure about what I am saying, think about the last meal you had. What was it made of? Where did it come from? How often did the presence of your mother hover over your plate? What is this empty plate you pushed away every single day of your childhood? I quit eating beans and tortillas and I am no longer swallowing the world on borrowed time.

WRITE

"It is time to write," he said, so I sat down, not knowing what I was going to write about. I looked up at him and he smiled, his features giving me ideas, but not pushing my hand to the notebook to set them down. I glanced over his shoulder and saw there was a Bozo the clown painting on the far wall. This was my office, after all, and I was stunned to see a framed picture I had not put on the wall. If he had mounted it there, I never saw him do it. He had been standing in front of my desk the whole time. Instead of being frightened, or thinking I was crazy, I looked at this man who wanted me to write and thought about a recent survey that said kids thought pictures of clowns were more frightening than hairy monsters or aliens. I thought of Bozo and tried to set something down on the page, but nothing happened. The man finally moved away from the window and the light that he let in hit the clown picture, setting it to glow as if fresh, newly invented paint had been used. I closed my notebook and leaned back in my chair. "Why do you want me to write?" I asked him, keeping my eyes on the smiling, wicked Bozo face on the wall. The man came close to my desk and looked down at me. "I want you to set down your deepest fears." I blinked a couple of times, stared at this man whose name I did not even know, and opened my notebook again. I waited for him to step back. As I started to write a few words with my pen, he went over to the painting and straightened the corners of the frame. It looked brighter now. I glanced back at the white page of my notebook, finished my sentence, then read it quietly back to myself. "When I was a boy, I was afraid of clowns." I looked up. The painting had disappeared from the wall. The man turned to look at me with a smile. "See what I mean?" he asked.

TRINITY

I am walking across the desert a few years after the world has ended. The entire landscape is white—mountains, arroyos, the rocks, even the dry cactus are white. I am near Trinity, the site of the first atomic bomb, White Sands, New Mexico. I come upon a slab of broken rock in my sandy path and see there is a tiny white lizard sunning itself. I squint up at the two suns in the sky and am glad it is a sunny day. When I look down at the lizard a second time, its white tail has fallen off its body and is floating a few inches off the ground. This frightens me, so I run. Dodging a growth of thick barrel cactus, I trip and fall down. As I land on my stomach, a fine cloud of white dust rises around my body, some of it falling on my hair, the rest hovering in the air as if a great desert sandstorm is about to begin. I get up slowly and look down at my cut left knee. I am bleeding white blood for the first time. I run again, knowing the river is close by, and come up over a rocky ledge and spot the long ribbon of white water below. I descend to the tall, white reeds of grass that line the riverbanks. As I step over them, trying to get to the water and take a drink, I hear the sound of merry voices. Parting the reeds, I find myself directly across from a white boat. It looks like a riverboat from the nineteenth century, but smaller. It is crowded with people—men and women in fine white tuxedos and evening gowns. The women shade their heads from the two suns with beautiful white umbrellas as the men take off their white top hats and point to me. It is the first time I have encountered anyone on the river. When I come to get water, no animal or human is ever around. I stand there and stare at them, then spot the letters printed on the side of the boat— Southwest Museum Tours. I begin to panic and fall back into the reeds, not wanting to hear what is coming over a loudspeaker on the boat. "And, over there, Ladies and Gentleman, one of the last survivors of the Great Event. As you can see, the species was native to the area hundreds of years ago. If we slow down and stop, he will appear again. It is known they come to the river every day to drink. There he is again. If you look carefully, you can see him running east. Unfortunately, our overland jeep tour is closed today, as we are having trouble finding gasoline. Otherwise, we would show you how he lives between here and those white mountains over there."

THE TRAIN

I buy a train and park it in my front yard. It has many cars and surrounds the neighborhood with old railroad cars. When I go sit in the engine compartment and pretend I am piloting the train, the neighbors hiss and throw things at me. I sit in the engine compartment a long time. The traffic on the street dies down because the train takes up all the parking spaces. When the cops come, I show them the empty caboose and they leave me alone. One night, I am awakened by the train whistle blasting across the dark trees. I jump out of bed shaking and run outside in my underwear. I notice a few lights in some houses going on. I climb quickly up the ladder to see who has blown the horn because I always lock the doors at night. This time, I find one open and step inside. The cold steel greets me in darkness. I reach the engineer's compartment, but there is no one there. I look everywhere, thinking a neighborhood kid stayed up late to break in and blow the whistle. I find nothing. As I sit back down on the engineer's high chair, the entire train shudders and begins to slowly move down the street. I don't know what to do. I don't know how to stop a train. I'm in the front engine car as it crushes two or three automobiles parked ahead of it. The screeching sound wakes the entire street, and I have an audience as the train picks up speed. By the time it snakes its way onto the freeway, the entire city has come alive, millions of lights getting out of my way as I head out of town, my bare shoulders cold in the wind, the engineer's greasy cap crooked on my head, the cigar I grabbed from my nightstand on the way out now lit, its dim red glow guiding me as I shovel and shovel more coal, on my way to show the world my working train.

CHURCH

A man walks into a church and finds he is the only person in the dark sanctuary. He goes to the altar where several votive candles are quietly burning. He stops in front of a peeling statue of La Virgen de Guadalupe, bows down before the shrine and makes the sign of the cross. Suddenly, a bat flies out of nowhere and streaks across the chamber. Startled, he follows the darting creature with his eyes as it disappears beyond the choir balcony. He turns back to the candles so he can pray, but is disrupted by a drop of water landing on his sleeve. He looks up at the distant ceiling in time for a second drop to hit him on the chin. It's raining outside and the roof is leaking. The man moves on his knees a couple of feet down the bench and begins his first Our Father. He is halfway through the prayer when an altar boy, mumbling incoherently, runs from the priest's chamber, his footsteps echoing through the church. The man is distracted again as the boy, dressed in his colorful frock, takes one of the small burning candles and returns to the back room. The man shakes his head at the trail of wax the boy drips on the floor. This time, he manages a complete Our Father and two Hail Marys before a dense cloud of incense fills the air around the statue. He begins to cough and his eyes start burning. He rises to his feet and notices the poison sweetness of the incense is coming from the priest's chamber. He coughs and walks back there, but the incense makes him nauseous and he stops at the door. Inside, the altar boy is holding the ugly bat over the candle flame, its wings folded so it won't escape. Next to him, an old priest is crying and shaking his head, his clothes soaked from the rain, a pot of incense hanging from a rope in his outstretched hand. The man turns and bolts down the long aisle between the pews. As he reaches the sanctuary doors, he spots the containers of holy water mounted on the walls. He can't resist and dips a finger in one of them, then raises the wet finger to trace a cross on his forehead. This sets off a loud clattering of wings behind him, but he does not turn to look. When he opens the door, it is early evening and the rain has stopped, everything under the sky wet and shiny. Hundreds of bats pour out of an open window below the bell tower. They fill the sky as the man stands under the arch, not quite sure where he parked his car. Three more altar boys come up the concrete stairs toward him and he gets out of the way as two priests embrace each other on the sidewalk near the street.

Freelie Vasquez owned 8,452 vinyl records, which
he kept on custom-built wooden shelves in the basement of his
house. His stereo system was cheap, Freelie spending his money on
records more than equipment, though his Sony turntable was a good
one that had lasted ten years with only a couple of needle changes.
His 8,452 albums ranged from fifties blues by Chicago musicians, to
late seventies British bands. He wouldn't buy any new music besides
that of giants like Dylan, Neil Young, or Van Morrison. His thing
was collecting old sixties and seventies vinyl of every imaginable and
obscure British and U.S. band—Help Yourself, Badger, Mick Abra-
hams, Gypsy, the original Oar by Skip Spence, plus hundreds of Beatles, Dylan, and Neil Young bootlegs. You name it, Freelie had it. He
bought albums at garage sales and used record stores, took them
home to play a few times and then filed them away—unless it was a
favorite like the Deep Purple album with Tommy Bolin, which he
wore out. Freelie was an expert at rock and roll trivia, but it was the
collecting more than the music that drove him and made his wife
divorce him. She walked out when he was stoned on reefer in the
basement, his third set of headphones on the carpet, receiver glowing in the dark as his favorite Jimi Hendrix bootleg, "Woke Up and
Found Myself Dead," that infamous jam with Johnny Winter and Jim
Morrison, crackled on the turntable. He owned four different press-
ings of the bootleg, each with a different cover. His job as a mail
sorter in the main post office allowed him to buy the vinyl he wanted,
but 36 years of buying records with little time for anything else, also
made Freelie a sick puppy because his kitchen and bedroom had not
been cleaned in months. The stink and garbage were reaching a
point where the neighbors were close to grabbing the phone and

reporting him. One night after Freelie left his basement window open and fell asleep to Morrison's drunk screaming, a neighbor, tired of the smell and the music, crept across the two foot high grass in Freelie's yard and tossed a smoke bomb and a stink bomb called "a worm" through the window. The smoke bomb rolled onto a cement section of the basement floor while the worm dropped onto the plastic cover Freelie placed on his turntable when not playing it. The smoke began to fill the room and the worm expanded into a long, black mess and started melting the plastic cover. Freelie jumped out of his ancient recliner and almost hung himself on the headphone cord, his long Robert Plant hair tangled in it. He yanked it off and screamed at the stinking smoke curling up and down the endless rows of neatly filed albums, all 8,452 of them inside plastic covers. He went berserk when he spotted the burning fireworks. There was no way Freelie was going to pour water in the basement or have time to get thousands of records out of there, so he did the next best thing and used his bare foot to stomp out the smoke bomb first, the stubborn thing refusing to go out because it was designed to burn that way. It stuck to the bottom of Freelie's foot and kept burning. He picked up an old *Rolling Stone* magazine with ZZ Top on the cover, and as he hated ZZ Top, he smashed the worm with it, flattening the burning chemical into the plastic cover, which only gave the stink more life. Freelie gagged in the clouded room, his foot on fire, his albums vanishing into the smoke. He couldn't imagine anything more frightening—not seeing his rows of albums. He owned at least twenty locks to cover doors and windows, but had been too careless to shut the basement tonight. The smoke and stink pushed Freelie against a row of Grateful Dead bootlegs. He reeled in agony over his foot, bounced off his Marianne Faithful albums, and fell into the row of 47 Dylan bootlegs. He screamed as the albums tumbled onto the floor, kicked out with his torched foot and left melting plastic on three copies of Moby Grape's first album—the one with the dude giving the finger to the cover photographer. Soon, that vinyl started its slow melt. Freelie crawled past his Frost LPs, pushed into a bottom corner of the shelf where his Peter Green imports stood, and lifted himself up the basement stairs. By this time, the smoke bomb had gone out, but clouds of smoke hung there. Freelie leaped onto the kitchen counter, threw old cans of tuna out of the sink, and stuck his foot in there. The water from the faucet hissed as Freelie sat on the counter and cried. He sobbed for a long time, and when he finally stirred from his stupor and opened his eyes, the smoke in the basement was barely visible. He heard an incredibly beautiful guitar solo echoing downstairs, its purity shaking the walls of his house. He leaped off the counter, ignoring his blistered and swollen foot, and limped to the basement doors. Suddenly, the stage lights exploded and thousands of people in the auditorium cheered. "Freelie! Freelie! Freelie!" they screamed and held burning matches in the pot atmosphere. Jimmy Page hugged Freelie and pointed to the white Stratocaster strapped around Freelie's shoulders. "Yeah, man!" Freelie heard Ringo Starr yell from behind the drums as Jack Cassidy and Jorma Kaukonen stepped away from the mike. Jerry Garcia was there, so was Janis, but Freelie was almost doubled over with the hurt he felt in his heart when he realized Jimi was not present. The crowd went wild as Freelie touched the Stratocaster, the feedback flying across 8,452 albums, stacks of foggy vinyl aligning themselves in neat rows as Freelie stepped into the spotlight, lifted the untouched cover to his turntable, and gently placed the dark vinyl onto the spinning wheel.

THE ORACLE
AND THE GREEN BIRD

After a painting by Wilfredo Lam

The green bird took history away when its wings danced around the oracle's body. The green bird with double beak spoke about double worlds—inventions of the mind where every woman who was made love to by a bird forgot the swan and took this secret greenery instead. The long white arm of the oracle reaches out and pinches the testicles of the green bird—a mighty portrait over her long, black robe—the bird's face not sure whether to show pleasure or the last gifts of life. She pinches it again and sorcerers fly beyond the piano notes that blend behind the lovers. The oracle's white face turns whiter, her pure white eyes looking straight ahead to see if the lovely world has ended yet so she can stay with her bird. The green bird embraces her and sees what the oracle has always seen—fresh four-legged beings crossing the river in search of nests, frozen carcasses of the last Gods who were abandoned by black widows floating stiff at the end of the continent. The green bird blinks again, the cool fingers of the oracle soothing his testicles so he won't be angry and will be able to decipher what she wants him to know. If you look closer, the oracle actually has three arms—one wrapped under the bird's body, the second pointing to something outside the picture—the third hanging limp at her side. An oracle with three arms and the green bird with two beaks. When the bird was young, its mother told him there would be years of escape and years of nests—swallowed songs and seasons without prey, vast journeys beyond the ice to find the black tree where the bird's father was burned centuries ago. A flugelhorn sounds and the hazy outline of another object in the painting focuses on the eye of the observer. It is a diamond shape with six horns, four more than the two that sit on the head of the oracle, her beautiful smile attracting flies, hidden danger, and the last man who painted green feathers on his back so he could fly. The diamond shape won't come to the forefront of the painting, hangs in the background behind a cloud Lam must have stolen from his family. The green bird tires of this magic and flaps its wings. When everyone stands back, an enormous wall of green and black covers what perception is allowed—the barrier climbed years ago when the oracle was given the gift and taken from her twin brother. The wall is here, reflecting what is seen and not accepted—what the green bird meant when it turned its head and plucked one eye out of the oracle, recalling how its mother dropped a worm into its hungry throat, hissed and scolded it, told the green bird the one-eyed woman was the source of his ability to fly.

THE WORLD IS FULL
OF TORTILLAS

Amparo wakes up and the world is full of tortillas. His bed in his grandmother's house is stacked high with fresh tortillas, so when he throws his blanket off, he knocks dozens of tortillas to the floor. It doesn't matter, because there are hundreds of tortillas already down there on the floor. Amparo sits up and the wonderful smell makes him hungry, though he is confused as to why his grandmother has thrown so many tortillas in his room. He gets dressed and goes into the kitchen where his grandmother, a short woman with long, white hair, is bent over the black stove, patting another tortilla onto the hot plate. Her table holds six towers of tortillas, each one at least two feet thick. Amparo knows enough about cooking tortillas to realize she has been doing this for hours, probably all night. He calls to the old woman, but she waves him off, pointing to his usual glass of milk on the edge of the crowded table. He takes his glass and watches her move to the counter where hundreds of masa balls are piled on a wooden slab. She takes one and kneads it with her bare hands and flattens it on the metate, then drops the wooden roller with a thud and moves to the stove. Each time she does this, she brings back a fresh, hot tortilla and sets it on a stack. Amparo can't believe it. He has never seen anything like this. He finishes his milk, but can see she won't be cooking his breakfast of fried eggs this morning. The kitchen is devoted to this invasion of tortillas. He would go play with his neighbor Tino, but it is raining. Before he decides what to do, an old man opens the front screen door and enters the house. Amparo has never seen him before and stares at the wet figure who smiles at Amparo as water runs over his grandmother's floor. She turns to the old man without a word, as if expecting him. The old man stands by the stove, but neither one speaks. Amparo sits in a chair waiting. His grandmother stops her cooking, picks up the hottest tortilla off the stove, and hands it to the old man. Amparo is amazed by the man's white hair which is almost as long as his grandmother's. The old man continues to drip water as he takes the tortilla and bites it hungrily. She waits for him to finish, even ignoring the burning tortilla on the stove. When he is done, she slaps him hard across the face. Amparo's eyes widen in shock as the old man reels, then straightens and takes a second slap. She grabs a handful of tortillas, drops two on the floor, and gives the rest to the old man. He takes the tortillas and tries to smile. "Get out of here," are the first words Amparo hears his grandmother say this morning. She waits with clenched fists at her side as the old man shuffles out into the rain. Amparo goes to the door and watches the old man bite another tortilla as he disappears into the rain. "Who was that, Grandma?" he asks, afraid of her anger. His grandmother stands beside him. 'That is your grandfather." "My grandfather?" Amparo says. "You told me he died before I was born." She rubs her grandson's head. Amparo looks out the door, but the man is gone. "I've never seen my grandfather on his birthday before." His grandmother goes back into the smokey kitchen and throws the burned tortilla in the trash. Amparo doesn't like the smell and decides to go outside. Before he leaves, he goes to the table to steal a tortilla, but stops when he sees an entire stack is missing. "Yes, Amparo," his grandmother continues with her back to the boy. 'Today is your grandfather's birthday and he always loved tortillas."

CLAPPING

Tato's grandfather told him it is good to clap your hands to keep the bad spirits from coming near you. Tato didn't know what his grandfather was talking about. They sat on the front porch of their house and the street was quiet, no cars kicking up dust or neighborhood boys running between the houses. In the bright sun of the morning, Tato's grandfather started clapping his large, wrinkled hands together. They echoed across the yard. "Where are the bad spirits coming from?" Tato asked, as he looked around without seeing anything unusual. His grandfather stopped clapping and looked sternly at Tato. "The loco will come get you when you don't even know he is there." He paused. "But, if you clap your hands every day, the loco will be a good spirit and help you with any problem you have." Tato didn't understand what his grandfather was saying, until that afternoon, when the rainstorm hit. He was playing by himself in the alley across the street, which ran between rows of boarded up adobe houses. Tato heard bad things happened in those houses, but he loved to go there and look at the graffiti and carvings that strangers left on the walls. The storm hit as Tato was trying to climb into one of the empty houses through an open window. He had been so enthralled by the graffiti, he did not notice the fast moving storm. The first roll of thunder cracked across the sky, frightening him, so that he lost his balance and fell into the room. The impact threw clouds of dust into the dark air. The room was very cold. Tato rose to his feet and wondered how he was going to get out and get home. As he reached for the open window, he heard the clapping behind him. For a split second, he thought it was his grandfather, but what would he be doing in the shadows? He turned quickly to find no one there. The musty smell in the room added to the echo as the handclapping started again. It seemed to come from the next room. Tato stepped carefully over fallen beams and piles of trash and made his way into the next room. There was no door to stop him. He was greeted by the continuing sound of someone clapping and called out in the dark, "Grandpa?" even though he knew it wasn't so. He heard a footstep and was surprised he had not run out of the scary room by now. Something moved in one of the black corners. Tato stared as a man emerged out of the wall. He was thin, brown skinned, and reminded Tato of his father, Antonio, who was away in the Army. The man was dressed in faded blue levis and a gray sweatshirt. He looked at Tato with a blank expression on his face. His crewcut added to Tato's sense he had seen this man before. As the silent figure came closer, a rough beam of light from a second broken window highlighted his features. The man not only looked like his father, but bore an even stronger resemblance to his grandfather as a young man, the way he looked in the old photographs Tato had seen. The image from those photos was standing before him. Before Tato could say anything or let his fear take over, the silent man clapped his hands. This time, the clapping did not make a sound. Tato's eyes widened as he stared at the clapping hands. Tato backed away a couple of feet and the man seemed to clap harder, his arms swinging wider, his open palms and fingers crashing together with a deafening silence. Tato shook his head, ran out of the room, leaped out the window where he first fell in, and ran home. When he reached the porch, his grandfather was rocking on the swing, waiting for him. "Grandpa!" Tato cried, out of breath. His grandfather stopped swinging, planted his sandaled feet on the ground, and hugged his grandson. Neither the boy or the old man said a word as the last roll of thunder cut across the neighborhood like a heavy handclap from heaven.

THE ROSARIES

He held the rosary in his hands and did not know what to do with it anymore. He had run out of prayers and had worn the black beads down to hard grains of shame and worry. The world was coming to an end and he did not know which of his prayers could prevent this. He sat on his bed and waited for something to happen outside the music of his chanting and yearned for someone to come through the door and tell him the threat was over, his prayers had been answered and he could put his dangling beads away. He held the rosary in his hands and the words to dozens of Our Fathers and Hail Marys rang in his head. He could not get rid of them even though he had stopped saying the rosary one hour ago. The chanting repeated itself over and over, the low sounds of guilt he had known all his life bouncing off the silence lodged in the back of his throat. He reached to the nightstand, took the glass of water, and sipped from it. The cold stream ran down his sore throat and the words "who art in heaven" rang in his ears. He thought he heard someone downstairs, but knew he was alone in the house. The others had gone to mass without him. They had invited him, but he told them he did not feel well and needed to get more sleep. When he woke, they were gone and he found his rosary on top of the nightstand. It had not been there last night when he got ready for bed. He always kept it inside a handkerchief tucked away in one of the drawers. When he was fully awake, he sat up, held the rosary in his hands and prayed two whole cycles, until he could not pray anymore. Now he folded it back into the handkerchief and closed the drawer. When he went to the window and looked out, he saw a line of people marching down the street. It was a large crowd of mourners slowly passing his house. Old men and women bundled in coats and shawls hung their heads in grief. Most of them were dressed in black and he could tell rosaries hung from their hands as they proceeded. He stepped away from the window and got dressed. By the time he got his shirt and pants on and tied his shoes, the mourners were halfway down the street. He wondered where they were going, because the church was in the opposite direction. He had not spotted a casket, so it could not be a funeral procession heading toward the cemetery. He hurried out of the house and walked briskly toward the crowd. When he approached two of the women at the end of the column, they turned toward him as if they were expecting him. Before he could ask them where they were going, the two women with their faces hidden by dark hoods handed him their rosaries. He had no time to hesitate as the two strings of warm beads were thrust into his hands. He stopped in the middle of the street and watched the mourners as they grew smaller and smaller in the distance. He could not follow because he now possessed two more rosaries. He turned back toward his house and hoped his family would not return from mass anytime soon. He went back into his bedroom, shivered because of the short minutes outside, and got back into bed without getting undressed. He set the two black rosaries on his nightstand, unfolded his own from the handkerchief, and set it next to the new ones. He lay down with his head on his tucked arms and stared at the rosaries. He reached for the closest one the women had given him, lay under the covers, and started to pray.

READING THE BOOK

Imagine the glow on your face sustaining itself, collecting amber remorse for the thought of retreat, opinion for the language of forgotten deeds where you belong and can't be driven away like the tiny statue of a prancing wolf floating away on a lily pad. Music mistakes itself for salvation and going there becomes a dance between insistence and the very thing that swallows the magic wand without becoming a wind-up toy trapped in a dark forest. Imagine how the fist in the water causes the landscape to become twisted— miles of trees burned down before anyone could discover the rest of the waiting world. How often have you thought about this before putting on your Nixon mask and walking into the office of your college president? How soon will the man and woman recognize their home and imagine themselves loving inside it every night? There is no wisdom when looking back involves reshaping the heart to fit itself. Love as a flugelhorn. Love as a spinning flower. Love as the saxophone constructed out of the old bones that disintegrated when the man and woman still loved each other. When one door is the hair that is parted, you step in and dwell there for many years, your best suits worn by your cousin's girlfriend. Pretend the fox and the coyote were the animals that sounded in the empty sleeve of your sleep. Pretend their tracks in the dirt look like the first steps you took when you abandoned those myths—stories told to you about weeping women, hungry dogs, and men with combs sticking out of their noses. They were all searching for you. In the picture book, someone cut out the image of the lizard and the snake—the coyote that swallowed shadows and became your brother walking the high wire without teeth. Is this the manner by which you close the book? Was there room for the man and woman to return and change the story they wrote in your pages? When they come back, you are their son reciting stories about the way they cut out your tongue, how the baby's diaper was changed after it peed—the milk given to them that fed the river as you dripped like the baby when you came out, making sounds no paws could follow toward the red splash of the driven heart.

THE BOUNDARIES
ARE THERE

First the friendly light must approach you without harming your lemon eyes or taking away your key chain of the seven monkeys. They laugh at the odor of bear and your casual drift toward the glacier where the pink fire continues to write. The second wind belongs to the seashell embedded in the early desert years of your vast childhood, the fossil falling out of the magnolia to warn you not to dig there. When the drummer pounds closer to your chest, you are on the right track toward painting the fourth eye on the bald forehead of a grandfather you never knew. When his parchment opens to the wrong scratch of the century, the one hundred years will take you and demonstrate how you were one of the men who walked the coast before the genocide. Green surface of turtles, iguanas, and brown waves of running figures met you at the highest fence where every other face on the totem pole was you and every other face was your father. The third wish must have been the keyboard dug out of your brain when they brought you in, the programmed notes creating a dance for the things you can't describe. Its keys are worn yellow to fit your eyes, the tunes it announces mistaken for something falling out of the sky to remind you there are boundaries. When you drink the clean water, something floats on its surface. One lick, and it flashes in your mind before you can lock the chain on your cheetah, its perfect teeth spelling danger that passed when you were born. One lick from the cat, and it flashes in your mind. The fourth house by the river is where you appear next, your knees now chambers where the wax child was held prisoner, its membrane of gold memory preserving the war until the day the button is pushed. It could be a demonstration. Instead, it is a dance with an old doorway, how it burned and never fell—the flames licking their own house to see what the world smelled like, making the ruins a historic place where they would find you alive someday. The fifth direction must be the slender tentacle of brilliance and your skill at staring through the wrong map of the remaining planet, guessing where the next terrorist attack will come, where the unknown woman is kidnapped and raised as a poetry nun. When you pinpoint the red and green lines in her notebooks, it will be the gate to the sixth sense—reflection and the escape given when you are allowed to make mistakes, forgiven for carrying three whistles made from the elbows of your father, the air they capture calling your name over and over as you wander the streets in search of a terrible painting. The seventh member of this story is not on the map. He is the guardian of the actual path—an icon prayed to by desperate, tattooed children tired of dancing the twist, wanting attention and flair, their style of breeding in the alleys influencing the economy—asking for strangers like yourself to drop coins or they will steal your clay pots of strange growths before you can see the eighth country of your home. When you find it, the ninth hand of your angry great-grandfather will greet you in your sleep and you will be given everything he lacked—speed and grace and the human touch necessary to count the tenth decade as the only period of a prosperous life left out of the official record of your existence and need.

THE WALLS

Julius Caesar's head was cut off and fed to the barbarians waiting outside the walls of Rome. Salvador Dali wore one orange sock and one white sock on days he went to eat breakfast in cafes. On days he stared at the wall, he did not wear socks. Yukio Mishima sheathed his knives in thick whale oil, claiming such creatures were the only ones who understood the art of sacrifice. The last thing John Lennon saw before he died from the gunshots was the brick wall of his apartment house. Sitting Bull had fourteen wives he lined up against the cliff walls. He closed his eyes, and walked blindly toward them with an erection, promising he would take the first one his hardness touched. Crazy Horse watched silently from the cliff walls above. J.D. Salinger scribbled on his bedroom walls as a boy, promising his mother to whitewash the figures the first time he was caught. Joan of Arc climbed over the walls and fell on top of a castle guard, the commotion bringing the soldiers who swore later the wall opened and she escaped by simply walking through. Nikita Kruschev stared at the wall of nuclear buttons and knew it was a green one they told him to push, but the triggers were every color except green. Hernan Cortes' men met a wall of arrows, turned and ran. Montezuma's men met a wall of armor, wept, then stoned their chief off the wall for helping the conquistadores. Carl Jung opened his eyes to find himself sleeping against a wall of flowers, the beautiful smell giving him the answer he had been looking for. Charlie Chaplin ordered his crew to remove the hidden mirror from the wall, footage of his latest lover overflowing onto the studio floor. Sor Juana de la Cruz hid her latest poem in a hole in the wall, but when a fellow nun went to retrieve it after Sor Juana' death, it was gone. The Dalai Lama stopped before the wall of snow and bowed his head to pray, the slain monks around him forming a wall of bodies. Virginia Woolf's final memory before she drowned was the wall of family portraits, the photographs of her father and brothers so radiant in the river fog. Billy the Kid simply cut a hole in the adobe wall of the jail with his bare hands and walked away. Janis Joplin was found dead of an overdose in her Los Angeles hotel, her face turned toward the wall. Federico Garcia Lorca did not face any walls when he was shot under the trees. No one knows how Tu Fu encased himself in a wall of bamboo, staying inside the tube for five years, never saying a word, his feet becoming the roots of bamboo within the first few months of his silence. Al Capone stared at the walls of his cell in Alcatraz and added the bank figures again, trying to get them right. Babe Ruth heard a thud against the wall of his hotel suite, the baseball rolling down the hallway as a signal his tryst with the team owner's wife was about to be revealed. William Shakespeare stared at the empty walls of the theatre, stood there without saying a word, and stared at the empty walls of the theatre. Geronimo extended his arms over the walls of rock, the approaching sound of the cavalry troops echoing down the canyon, the pictograph Geronimo carved high on the wall, years ago, lifting him to safety. Two days before Salvador Allende was gunned down, Pablo Neruda, dying of cancer, woke at Isla Negra to find the walls of the room where he lay covered in hundreds of clinging starfish.

RAY GONZALEZ is a poet, essayist, and editor born in El Paso, Texas. He is the author of *Memory Fever* (University of Arizona Press, 1999), a memoir about growing up in the Southwest, *Turtle Pictures* (Arizona, 2000), which received the 2001 Minnesota Book Award for Poetry, and a collection of essays, *The Underground Heart: Essays From Hidden Landscapes* (Arizona, 2002). He is the author of six other books of poetry, including three from BOA Editions—*The Heat of Arrivals* (1997 PEN/Oakland Josephine Miles Book Award), *Cabato Sentora* (2000 Minnesota Book Award Finalist), and *The Hawk Temple at Tierra Grande* (2002). His poetry has appeared in the 1999 and 2000 editions of *The Best American Poetry* (Scribners) and *The Pushcart Prize: Best of the Small Presses* 2000 (Pushcart Press). His non-fiction is included in the second edition of *The Norton Anthology of Nature Writing* (W.W. Norton). He is the editor of twelve anthologies, most recently *Touching the Fire: Fifteen Poets of the Latino Renaissance* (Anchor/Doubleday Books, 1998). He has served as Poetry Editor of *The Bloomsbury Review* for twenty-two years and founded *LUNA*, a poetry journal, in 1998. Among his awards are a 2000 Loft Literary Center Career Initiative Fellowship, a 1998 Illinois Arts Council Fellowship in Poetry, a 1993 Before Columbus Foundation American Book Award for Excellence in Editing, and a 1988 Colorado Governor's Award for Excellence in the Arts. He is an Associate Professor in the MFA Creative Writing Program at The University of Minnesota in Minneapolis.